THE CLIENT'S CONUNDRUM

A VEGAN VAMP MYSTERY

CATE LAWLEY

For CRJ, who's always ready to brainstorm and is fascinated by the endless possibilities of magical worlds

ALSO BY CATE LAWLEY

VEGAN VAMP

Adventures of a Vegan Vamp

The Client's Conundrum

The Elvis Enigma

The Nefarious Necklace

DEATH RETIRED

Death Retires

THE GOODE WITCH MATCHMAKER

Timely Love

Ghostly Love

Deathly Love

Forgotten Love

The Goode Witch Matchmaker Collection

Writing as Kate Baray

LOST LIBRARY

Lost Library

Spirited Legacy

Defensive Magic

Lost Library Collection: Books 1-3

Witch's Diary

Lost Library Shorts Collection

The Covered Mirror: A Lost Library Halloween Short

Krampus Gone Wild: A Lost Library Christmas Short

SPIRELLI PARANORMAL INVESTIGATIONS

Spirelli Paranormal Investigations Season 1

Entombed: A Spirelli Investigations Novel

Writing as K.D. Baray

BEAUREGARD

Mistaken: A Seth Beauregard Short

BONUS CONTENT

Interested in bonus content for the Vegan Vamp series? Subscribe to my newsletter to receive a bonus chapter for *Adventures of a Vegan Vamp* as well as release announcements and other goodies! Sign up at http://eepurl.com/b6pNQP.

1

WHERE'S THE BATHROOM?

The woman at the front of the room smiled in that bland, uninterested way that people do when they've given a presentation fifteen times too many and didn't care whether you were listening or not. At least she had a pleasant voice.

"I know that some of you are new to the area and some of you are new to enhanced living."

Did she just look at me? I couldn't be the only newbie in the room. I shot a covert look around the room. Three rows of people, each with five seats. And with only two empty seats, that meant thirteen people in orientation. Nah, I couldn't be the only newbie.

"I've provided each of you with a binder. Inside the binder you'll find..."

Pleasant or not, it all sounded like blah, blah, blah. This was going to be an ordeal. And to think I'd been looking forward to the Society's official orientation ever since I found out one existed.

The thick binder in my hands was printed with the words "Property of the Society for the Study of Occult and

Paranormal Phenomena. Do Not Remove from Society Headquarters." Well, if you're going to give a girl—vamp—a handbook, you better expect her to take it home.

I wasn't sure how I'd lug three pounds of paper products and a massive 1990s-era binder out unnoticed, but I'd work it out.

Just as the presenter was getting to the good part—the location of the several bathrooms scattered throughout the warehouse facility—someone's phone rang. Shame on them. A lady needed to know where the facilities were located; you never knew when you'd have a makeup emergency or a wardrobe failure. Because as many fluids as I drank these days, I never seemed to actually need to pee. The wonders of magic.

The phone kept ringing. At some point—three rings later? five?—I realized I'd changed my ringtone...to that exact same one.

I dug through my purse, considered very briefly silencing the call, then answered, "Just one second."

I started to crawl over the feet and purses of those unfortunate enough to be seated in my aisle. The Society had packed us in like sardines, which was silly with the number of people attending. Just give us a bigger room.

"So sorry," I said to the woman whose foot I'd just trod on.

"Mallory?" I could just make out Gladys's voice on the phone, but I could hardly listen to her, crawl over strangers in a tight space, and make my apologies to the injured.

Even though she was my first and only afterlife coaching client, Gladys would have to wait.

Finally, I reached the end of the row and turned to give the presenter an apology wave, only to find her glaring at me. Oops. I waved and smiled anyway then stepped out into the hall.

"I'm so sorry, Gladys. It's just that today is—"

"I found a dead body in my bed."

I closed my eyes and sighed. I checked that no one was in the hall before I said, "Did you say dead? Next to you? In bed? Calm down. I'm on my way." I ended the call with another sigh.

Lord above, Gladys had turned into a project. She was probably having nightmares again. Although it had been a little while since she'd had one, so maybe... No, it had to be a nightmare. I headed toward the front of the warehouse building, to the retail shop Bits, Baubles, and Toadstools. It was the closest exit to the parking lot, and the stock in the store was always entertaining.

I'd helped Gladys through a rough few days when she'd first transitioned. Like me, she'd been bitten and accidentally turned into a vampire. Our progenitor—a nasty creature who'd been hanged for his crimes—had been gorging on the blood of women he'd found particularly annoying. In the midst of that, he'd killed several women (not a Society crime), but he'd also turned loose a few baby vamps on the world—and we'd been distinctly noticeable in our untrained dismay (definitely a Society crime).

Gladys and I were the only survivors, so far as I knew. The rest of the women he'd attacked had died. I had no memory of my particular neck-biting trauma, but Gladys remembered small pieces. And since then, men made her very uncomfortable. We'd been working on it. As her undead life coach, it was my job. Gladys might be my first client, but she seemed to be making great progress.

My cell pinged with a new text message. As I slid my finger across the screen, a photo popped up. I flipped my phone to enlarge the picture...yes, definitely a corpse. Definitely in a bed. Given our earlier conversation, most likely Gladys's bed.

I started at a jog—considered how that corpse might have ended up there—then ran.

As I sprinted to the front of the building, I couldn't help thinking at least he was a man. The implied sexual nature of their relationship—naked and in her bed, so one could assume—was evidence of her improvement. Unless, of course, she had something thing do with how he came to be no longer living.

Nah.

Either way, a dead body meant reinforcements were necessary. I made a beeline for my favorite investigator-enforcer-knight's office. Dead bodies usually meant all sorts of mess. Political mess, physical mess, maybe even magical mess.

Alex was great with messes and highly unlikely to turn me away. He liked me. That, and we shared a sensitive secret.

I arrived slightly out of breath at his office door. Whatever Alex might say about normal vamp behavior, *I* got out of breath when I ran. Knocking lightly produced no result, so I pounded.

"What?" It sounded like Mr. Cranky Pants woke up on the wrong side of the bed.

"It's Mallory." I opened the door to find a half-naked Alex rolling off the futon he used for emergency kip.

A lot of very nice, very naked chest, but surprisingly—that naked chest was covered in tattoos. Symbols, not pictures. And maybe letters? I leaned closer—

"What do you want?" He snatched a T-shirt off the side

table and pulled it over his head. I got a glimpse of his shoulders and back, also covered with the odd designs.

And most interesting of all, the T-shirt he'd thrown on covered every single bit of ink. No wonder I'd never noticed his tats before.

"Ah, my client woke up next to a dead body. Any chance you could help a girl out?"

It said a lot about our relationship that he didn't look terribly surprised. "I need fifteen minutes."

"Perfect," I said, even though fifteen minutes seemed like a terribly long time when a corpse was involved. "You're a complete doll."

He spared me a quick glare before disappearing into the bathroom. The door closed with a loud, firm click.

I knew how important his sleep was to him. That was one half of the secret we shared. The spirits—or demons or elementals; he hadn't really explained the difference—messed with him when he wasn't a hundred percent. As a result, Alex was a bit of a health nut. *How* exactly they messed with him, I didn't know. We hadn't shared quite that much.

Which led to the other half of the secret. Alex hadn't exactly shared that information. I'd seen one of the little nasties clinging to his back in the middle of the night. Apparently, sleep deprivation wasn't good for staving off the nasty critters.

Alex cracked the door, and I could hear water running. "Who's your client?"

I scrunched up my nose and hoped for the best. "Gladys Pepperman."

His groan was loud enough that I heard it over the running water. I waited—then let out a sigh of relief when he didn't say anything.

Alex poked his head out of the bathroom. "Aren't you supposed to be in orientation?"

I shrugged.

"Did you even go?"

"I went. I can even tell you where all of the bathrooms are."

He stuck his head out again, but this time he was brushing his teeth, so he shot me an exasperated look. "So you pee now?"

"None of your business. A woman—vamp or otherwise—is allowed to retain a little mystery about personal habits."

"That's a no, then?"

I shifted the large orientation binder from one arm to the other. "That's a no. Hey, I don't suppose theft of orientation materials is one of those crimes that leads to swift execution by hanging?"

Something clattered in the bathroom and Alex swore.

"You okay in there?"

"Yes." And not long after, he exited looking brighter-eyed—and wearing a small piece of toilet tissue on his jaw. "You will not be hung for stealing orientation materials. But bring them back. There's some sensitive information inside."

"And no witchy protection spells that do something nasty—like soak me in dye or make me smell funky—when I cross the headquarters' threshold?"

"No, but it's a thought if we keep getting made Society members like you."

Made versus born—was that what he meant? Such a bizarre prejudice, but groups will hyper-focus on the differences. Alex was born, naturally. Or perhaps he wasn't referencing my made status but was simply commenting on my uniquely irreverent attitude.

"Ready?" When he nodded, I chucked my keys at him. He had a thing about driving, so I let him. As the more flexible individual in the relationship, it seemed the right thing to do. And Alex's enhanced dexterity and speed meant he had mad driving skills.

"Oh." I pulled up the picture on my phone as he locked his office. "This is the guy."

He glanced at my phone then closed his eyes. When he opened them, he snatched my phone and examined the picture more closely.

"This is the CEO of the Society."

"No." I knew that guy, and this wasn't that guy. "Cornelius has a beard. And he's shorter, stockier."

"Cornelius is the chief *security* officer. This is the chief *executive* officer."

"Oh." I thought about it. "Uh-oh."

Alex ran his hand through his hair. "Uh-oh is a massive understatement."

2

DEAD MEN MAKE ICKY HERBS

"I rolled over, and he was just there—dead. And naked." Gladys flashed big brown eyes at Alex.

She really had gotten much better with men. Much more so than I'd known, if the dead body and now her interaction with Alex were any indication.

"So you had..." I raised my eyebrows. "With Mr...."

Nuts. I'd forgotten to get the CEO's name.

"I don't know his name. And I didn't have sex with him." Gladys seemed shocked. "I didn't know him."

"Why was he in your house?" I asked. No delicate way to say it, really.

"That's what I'm trying to tell you: I don't know."

"I think Ms. Pepperman is trying to say that when she went to bed last night—alone—Mr. Dyson was not in her home. Is that right?"

Alex gave Gladys an encouraging smile.

"Yes." She smiled back. "Yes. That's it. Well done."

Alex had some strange power over women—even deeply traumatized ones, it seemed. I'd never asked him about it—because we weren't *that* close—but I wondered if it was some special wizard effect. I was still a little fuzzy on what enhancements were typical for each group in the Society's community. My temporary vamp roommate Wembley could be at turns quite expansive and very close-mouthed, depending on his mood, the moon cycle, the weather, the clothes he was wearing, and who knew what other criteria. The men in my life were particularly mysterious since I'd vamped out a few weeks ago and joined the Society.

"Okay. I understand. But..." I paused, wrestling with the delicate issue. "Where exactly is Mr. Dyson now?"

"I couldn't leave him here on my good sheets."

"Absolutely," I agreed, thinking perhaps something had gone awry in the transformation process and fried a few of Gladys's brain cells. It wasn't the first time I'd had the thought. "But where is he?"

"I buried him in the backyard."

It wasn't that she wasn't clever. Gladys was quite sharp. It was just that her reasoning sometimes took an unusual path.

I tried to remember that as I continued to drag information out of her. "I see. Do you remember where?"

A tiny wrinkle formed between her perfectly plucked eyebrows. "Of course. How could I forget? Come outside, and I'll show you."

"That would be helpful," I said.

Alex and I followed Gladys outside. She pointed to a perfectly groomed bed edged out with large stones. Inside the bed were newly planted herbs. "Those two are mint. And that's lavender, lemon balm, rosemary, basil, and parsley."

"You planted an herb garden. A fragrant and very edible garden." I spotted several neatly stacked plastic pots, the kind that plants came in from the nursery. "On top of Mr. Dyson."

Alex rubbed his face. "Gladys—"

I touched his arm. "You did all of that in between calling me and when we arrived?"

"No. That wouldn't be possible, would it?" Now she looked at me like I was the one short a few marbles. "I already had the plants from a few days ago. I've been planning this garden for weeks now, since before...you know. Anyway, I had the plants and mulch, and then there was the body."

"Right. And your sheets," I said.

"Exactly. But I definitely buried him before I called you. Why do you think I sent you a photo?"

Again—she wasn't an idiot, merely an original thinker.

"I'm not sure—why don't you tell us?" I glanced at Alex to make sure he was keeping mum. I was quite proud of myself. He'd have kicked me in the shin if our roles were reversed.

"The picture is to identify the victim. You can't solve the crime without knowing who the victim is...can you? I heard all about how you found our progenitor, so you're basically like a detective." Gladys cocked her head.

It was more accurate to say I was on the bad guy's trail when he found me—but who was I to quibble? Gladys thought I was a sleuth, and that was a teensy-weensy bit flattering. "Okay, so, you get that we have to dig him up now? Right?" I was trying to be gentle, trying not to point out the absolute lunacy of her actions, but once again she was looking at me like I just didn't get it.

"Wait a second." Alex considered the bed, the yard, the surrounding area. "Any chance your neighbors heard you doing anything unusual?"

If he was thinking about jumping on board with Gladys's whacky plan, then maybe I was the crazy one.

"I don't think so. I was really careful—and very quiet."

Alex indicated the six-foot fence. "No two-story houses, privacy fencing all around, large yards. It's possible no one saw anything."

I glared at him and pointed to the pretty herb garden. "Dead body."

"Just a second, Gladys." He pulled me away from Dyson's slowly rotting corpse and Gladys. He leaned close, speaking quietly. "Yes, it was an insane thing to do. But it's done. And he's the *CEO* of the Society. You do realize how important he is in local politics, right? Your client admits to being in bed with his corpse, is known to have violent reactions to men, and covered up the crime."

"I get that it looks bad. But there's no way Gladys did this. And if she did, she'd have told me. It's not like she's holding back now. And she's much better with men." I poked him in the chest. "Obviously."

"It's not my fault that I'm woman crack."

"Okay, that's clearly not true—but your...whatever it is you have is really annoying." I blew out a breath, considering his proposal. "You think they'll crucify her."

"Don't *you*?"

I looked at Gladys, now inspecting her nails, calm as you please. She was probably looking for grave dirt. "She hauled that body out here all by herself." I shook my head. "But, yes, I do think they'd hang her in a heartbeat. Assuming that killing people within the Society is actually a crime?"

"Yes, murder of a Society member is a crime. It's possible the occasional escalating feud is overlooked, but not the murder of a political figure." Alex eyed me. "You know most vamps aren't quite as wimpy as you."

"Say that when I have my magic sword with me, buster." Tangwystl was a personality-filled, living sword with a bloodthirsty streak. A gift, of a sorts, from my roommate. And I was sure once I learned how to use a sword I would be a kick-butt ninja sword-wielding vamp. I sniffed—that really was neither here nor there. And I couldn't believe it, but I was considering this completely harebrained scheme. "All right, let's say we do this. What's the next step?"

"Well, I do have a place in mind where we can stash him, but I need to check on that. Until then..."

If there was a wall near, I'd be banging my head on it. It looked like Dyson was going to be herb garden food. "All right. For now, he stays. And then?"

"We make sure that someone notices Dyson has disappeared. Shouldn't be hard; the guy is a workaholic." Alex grinned. "Then we get Cornelius to hire us to find him."

I laughed. But with a note of hysteria. "We perpetuate the myth of his disappearance then get paid to find him? You see no moral quandary with that? Not to mention that Cornelius will likely pluck our eyelashes bald if he catches a whiff of what's actually happening."

"He's more likely to have some toenails removed, but it's that or throw Gladys to the wolves." He tipped his head in her direction. "Deception is less of a moral quandary when you consider the alternatives."

Gladys was merrily adding potting soil to her newly made bed. No thoughts of swinging from a noose had entered her head; not that I could tell.

"Ugh. All right. Fine. But we have to find some way to convince Gladys to keep her mouth shut."

Alex and I turned back to Gladys. I couldn't help eyeing the herbs with misgiving. Enhanced dead guy decomposing and feeding their hungry little roots. Ick. I whispered to Alex, "What kind of enhanced being was Dyson?"

"Golem."

I shook my head. Sounded familiar, but I couldn't remember the particulars.

"They're made. Created from the dead flesh of unenhanced humans."

That's right. Now I remembered, and wasn't surprised I'd mentally blocked out those particular details. Double ick. Wembley said they tended to be pretty good-looking, because the mom and dad could pick and choose the parts. Triple ick.

As we approached, Gladys patted into place the last little bit of soil she'd added. "Isn't it nice? I've been wanting one for a long time."

Gladys had been recently divorced when she was turned. She'd finally escaped a controlling relationship with a type-A, overachieving, critical spouse, and not but weeks later was drugged, bitten, and unwillingly transformed into a vamp. She'd gone through a lot. Knowing that made it easier to deal with her particular quirks.

"I thought the mint would be nice for mojitos. And I hear that blood tastes heavenly with a small quantity of basil, parsley, and rosemary crushed and added right before you drink it."

I swallowed and tried not to ralph on the spot.

"Oh, I'm sorry." Gladys gave me a concerned look. "I forgot about your phobia. I shouldn't mention blood when you're around, should I?" She whispered "blood" as if lowering her voice made the word less offensive.

Right, because it was the mention of blood and not the herbs grown in a decomposing golem-man that was freaking me out. Actually, she wasn't wrong. The blood part was gross, too.

But I dredged up a smile. "Not a phobia, more a strong dislike. And yay! No more projectile vomiting. I've got that totally under control. But about..." I tipped my head in the direction of the herb garden, a.k.a. Dyson's resting place. "If Alex and I are going to be able to investigate, we need you to keep a low profile. And forget everything that's happened with Dyson."

"For now," Alex said.

"Who's Dyson?" She smiled innocently at me. Then she plucked a sprig off one of the plants and offered it to me. "Mint?"

She had the composure of an amazing liar, which was a little nutty given the situation...or brilliant. I couldn't figure out which.

3

ORIENTATION 0, MALLORY 1

I got in the passenger seat of my Grand Cherokee. I wasn't sure why we were in my car, other than I'd offered. Although I supposed Gladys had technically been *my* client. Not anymore.

"What's the grin for?" Alex asked.

"Just happy to share the Gladys burden. She's exhausting."

"Isn't she your first client? Your only client?"

I gave him my mean, squinty look—which appeared to have no impact. "That doesn't mean she's any less difficult."

"Just saying, without some comparisons... Never mind."

From the route we were taking, I guessed we were headed to the Society's headquarters. "Are we off to have a chat with Cornelius?"

"*You're* going back to orientation. I'm going to discreetly inquire as to Dyson's schedule for the day. Someone will notice his absence; he's an important, busy guy. And I'd like to have some idea when that's going to happen. Maybe nudge it along, if he's not missed soon." Alex looked me over head to foot. "Where's your orientation manual?"

"Ah." Since I wasn't sure, I did a quick look around, then remembered stashing it in the back. "Back seat."

"Uh-huh. Don't lose it."

"I won't." I tried to sound annoyed by the very idea, but since I'd actually forgotten where the thing was, I might have failed. "So, what are the chances Cornelius will actually hire us if Dyson's disappearance goes public?"

It was always good to be prepared when dealing with Cornelius. He was a stinker—a former despot (or so I suspected) turned bureaucrat.

"Exceptional. Cornelius trusts me."

That didn't seem particularly clever of the guy, since Alex had no problems lying to his boss. But I figured that refraining from comment was wisest. And I was pretty proud of myself. I was starting to think a little before I spoke, a big improvement for me. My transformation to vamp really had done a number on my impulse control.

"Can you give me some context for Dyson's role in the Society?" I asked. "I get that his title was CEO, but in terms of the enhanced community—what role did he play?"

Alex considered the question—or he was hyper-focused on his driving. Eventually, he said, "A small city or large town mayor, if you consider the enhanced population in Austin alone is around ten thousand, and he covers the whole state. So, yeah, a lot like a mayor."

"And if he's such a workaholic, why have I never seen him?" I asked, because I was no stranger to the Society's headquarters.

"He works primarily from his home out in West Austin."

West Austin could mean a lot of things, but it might mean he was loaded.

"Yes, since you're about to ask, he has money. And I have no idea if he could have been killed for it."

I hadn't quite made it so far as motive—but no reason to tell Alex that. "Any family that might inherit?"

"A wife. I'm not sure how they're getting along these days. I've never met her but heard rumors it wasn't a completely peaceful marriage. There's a daughter, as well, so I don't even know if she's in line for the bulk of the estate or if the daughter is."

"Anything else on the family?"

He tipped his head, and if I wasn't mistaken was looking ill at ease. "I've rarely seen Dyson over the last few years, and before that I was out of town. I'm not a good resource for that crowd, although I used to know Rachael, the daughter. I'd be surprised if she had anything to do with Dyson's death."

"I thought you'd been here a while." Except I couldn't remember why I thought that.

"Hm. I was, and I left, then came back."

"I'm a little surprised you're not tight with the CEO of the Society. You seem...well-integrated."

Alex glanced at me and gave me a crooked smile. "I don't exactly run in the same circles as Dyson. I'm also pretty sure that he never gave me a second thought beyond being the Society's landlord for headquarters."

"You own the warehouse?"

Alex looked at me in confusion. "I thought you knew that."

"Didn't have a clue. I know Bits, Baubles, and Toadstools is yours, but I assumed you rented the space."

He shook his head. "No. I bought the property ages ago, and when the Society needed a new space for headquarters, it turned out to be a good fit. But if you're done delving into my life..." He didn't take his eyes off the road, but I could feel his smirk from across the car.

Just because I expressed a little interest, the schlub made all sorts of assumptions. "Your ego is ginormous."

"Possibly."

During the tail end of the drive, I considered whether to quiz him about the metamorphosis of the language used to describe his job. Blade, knight, enforcer—most recently emergency response. But I'd already increased his ego by a factor of ten, and I was sure he'd think I was digging even more into his background. Take advantage of his unusual talkative streak? Or keep the man's massive ego in check?

As I considered the pros and cons, it occurred to me how odd the new terminology was. Emergency response. What a name, and very misleading. I snorted. They'd help you out... or kill you, depending on the emergency.

Not exactly EMS or the fire department or the police, the Society's emergency response unit was a weird combo of all three with a dash of executioner thrown in for fun. Maybe I was a little sensitive, but it was hardly surprising. I might have been an emergency response casualty had things gone differently with my vamp transformation.

"Any particular reason you're cracking yourself up over there?" Alex asked

Calling the Society's version of 911 should be a no-brainer in a pinch, but I'd sure think twice about it. Not funny.

"More hysteria than humor." Alex looked at me like I was an odd bug, so I changed the topic. "What's my story for leaving orientation?"

"The truth. You had a demanding client call you with an emergency. I doubt anyone will ask."

"Right." But as we drove through town, I couldn't shake the image of Dyson under those herbs. "You know, there is the possibility that Dyson's demise was from natural causes."

Alex snorted. "He's a golem."

"And that means what, exactly?"

"Natural causes are extremely unlikely. Also, why stash the body at Gladys's house if it wasn't murder?"

"Yeah, guess so," I mumbled.

Poor Gladys. But I didn't have long to feel sorry for her, because we arrived at headquarters a few minutes later.

We pulled into the parking lot, and I figured Alex was right: no one would ask where I'd gone. They were all too busy evacuating the building.

There were at least twenty, maybe thirty people milling around in the parking lot. "Don't suppose there was a fire drill planned for this morning," I said.

"No. And for this to happen on the day of Dyson's disappearance... I hate coincidences."

"Drama at the Society's headquarters and the Society's head honcho getting offed, all within ten or twelve hours? Nope, not a coincidence." I rubbed my hands together. "Ooooh. Another motive: some nefarious political maneuver. This sleuthing stuff is exciting."

Alex pulled the key out of the ignition and handed it to me. "Not to quash your happy, because I know how you feel about that, but you do realize that we've assisted in covering up a capital crime."

If Tangwystl were here, she'd blow a raspberry at him. I was much more mature than that, or I used to be and could still fake it when necessary. "Let's not get caught, then."

"Always the plan—just thought you'd lost sight of the bigger picture."

"If I've learned anything recently, it's that there is joy to be had in the little moments. So give in; experience the moment. You have to admit it's a little exciting to have two motives already, isn't it?"

"How about I just say that I'm pleased that you're pleased—and I'll keep pulling you back to the main path if you stop and sniff too many roses."

But the roses smelled so good.

I sighed. "Fair enough." I hopped out of the Jeep. Time to put on a show. I stopped midstride and almost tripped. "Whoa. Is that a bomb dog? I don't do bombs. Do I? I mean, a bomb would kill me dead, just like a normal human, right?"

"That's my bet, but you are one of a kind."

The dog was in a bright orange and black harness. It looked like a bloodhound...sort of. Not quite like in the movies. A little taller, leaner, generally more athletic but with the same long, droopy ears and sad expression. Whatever it was, if it was looking for explosives... "Nope. Not risking that."

Alex put a hand gently on my back and then shoved. "Come on. It's not a drug dog. Not exactly. Besides, since when have you seen a bloodhound drug dog?"

"Not *exactly*? How is 'not exactly' supposed to make me feel better?"

"It—he, actually—belongs to one of the Society members. He's got a good nose. I'm betting he's here looking for *someone* not *something*."

"Oh!" We'd moved in closer to the milling crowd, so I stopped myself just in time from mentioning Dyson. I huddled closer to Alex and lowered my voice. "But couldn't they just ask you? Your...you-know-what have eyes inside the headquarters, right?"

Alex pressed his lips together and pulled me further away from the crowd. "My you-know-what aren't exactly common knowledge, and Cornelius knows they're fickle creatures. Besides, Boone's completely reliable. Celia, the handler, is a djinni; she has a mind-to-mind connection with him."

"Mind control?"

"No," Alex snapped. In a more neutral tone, he said, "No. That's taboo, even with animals. I'm sure you can imagine why. She has a connection. Think of it like enhanced communication."

"With a dog?" I tried to envision that—but came up a blank. Bad enough with two different languages, but different species? No way. My brain hurt thinking about it.

"Yeah. It's a djinn thing. Point is, she'll get a good read from the dog on how long ago anyone who might be missing was in the building."

"Ah." I waved at the trim, bearded man headed our way. "Cornelius has spotted us."

Cornelius Lemann, CSO of the Society and generally the guy in charge of stuff, wasn't my biggest fan. Not a hater, and grateful I'd helped put a stop to the killing machine who'd transformed me, but probably just as happy if I didn't exist. I actually liked him, unlike my roommate who found him deeply untrustworthy.

I smiled at him. "Good to see you, Cornelius."

"I saw you two days ago, but thank you." He glanced over his shoulder at the milling people. "Here for orientation?"

I smiled.

"What's going on?" Alex asked.

"Dyson missed an appointment with me this morning. Since he called the meeting, his absence is noteworthy."

"And he's a stickler for etiquette," Alex said.

That was a tidbit Alex had omitted. I raised my hand.

Cornelius frowned at me. "What?"

"Was he the one behind the recent changes the Society has been making?" Both men looked confused. "Emergency response? More bureaucracy, less head chopping."

"Ah." Cornelius looked decidedly unhappy answering the question. "He was an active participant in all major decisions."

An obnoxiously bureaucratic non-answer, if ever I'd heard one. If it wouldn't put me in the hot seat to blow a raspberry at the police chief—the role Cornelius basically filled in the community—I'd have considered it. But I didn't need Cornelius too focused on me and my non-attendance at orientation.

Alex turned to face Cornelius more directly, basically cutting me out of the conversation. "Debrief me in your office? Mallory has to get back to orientation."

"Orientation is being rescheduled. Staff are just telling the attendees." Cornelius waved a dismissive hand in the direction of the milling crowd.

I resisted the urge to pump my fist. Probably not a diplomatic move in front of the guy whose division organized the thing. And really, I'd been excited about it...initially.

My joy must have leaked through, because Alex gave me a warning look. "I'm sure Becky will have it up and running in no time, although Dyson's absence is surely a concern to her."

"Looks like the masses are swarming to their cars." Cornelius gestured to the building. "Yes, yes. Quite a concern, I'm sure. They've worked together for decades."

My ears perked up. When I heard the name, it clicked. Becky was the presenter from my orientation this morning. I hadn't paid much attention at the time, but now she was a potential source. A somewhat bland, pedantic source, and likely one with a very poor first impression of me—but still, a source.

Two motives and a source already. This sleuthing thing was coming right along.

I swallowed a squeak of surprise. Alex had managed to follow Cornelius and kick my shin at the same time. The man had an absolute talent for knocking my shins. We needed to work on a subtler form of communication. I couldn't blame the guy—I'd been about a half second away from a little cheer. Cornelius might have wondered.

There was a reason I thought the transformation might have something to do with Gladys's peculiarities. Before my transformation, I'd been an anxiety-ridden, overachieving, neat-freak buzzkill. I mean, post-transformation I was still me, but without all of that anxiety. And while I liked my new afterlife coaching gig and the sleuthing was pretty fun, I was pretty sure I didn't qualify as an overachiever. I was tidy, but barely. I liked to think I wasn't a buzzkill anymore, but the jury was still out. I had basically three friends—and since Alex might not return my friendly sentiments, that number was probably closer to two. About Wembley and Bradley, I had no reservations. Those guys were solidly in the buddy camp. Alex was reliably in *my* camp—just not necessarily a buddy.

As I trotted behind Cornelius and Alex—who'd left me in the proverbial dust—my stomach decided it was a good time to be particularly loud in its protests. The bottomless pit that my stomach had become was another side effect of my transformation. I pulled out a bottle of vegetable juice I'd stashed in my purse and, once I was inside Bits, Baubles, and Toadstools—the retail store front of the Society's headquarters—I stopped long enough to chug half of it.

Better to appease the beast, otherwise I'd just get

hungrier and hungrier—and maybe a little cranky. Oh, and the embarrassment of descending fangs was something I really liked to avoid. My tiny baby fangs were embarrassing enough, but then they'd poke out when I was really hungry. Eek. A social gaffe of the most embarrassing kind.

"Hey!" I was about to get locked out of the backside of the building—where all the good stuff happened. I shoved my foot in the crack and grabbed the handle of the door marked "Employees Only."

4

ROSES AND WITCH HATS

I was surprised once again at the size of Cornelius's office. It was maybe a third the size of Alex's. Although knowing that Alex owned the entire building did provide a new context. And Alex did sometimes sleep in his office—like last night. I couldn't envision Cornelius crashing on a futon in the corner.

I sat down in the indicated chair, not entirely sure how I'd managed to sneak into this meeting. But if I stayed really quiet, maybe Cornelius wouldn't boot me out.

Alex sat down and said, "I'm not on call, so this is outside the realm of my duties as an emergency responder."

It was a weird way to start a conversation that we hoped would lead to us—or at least him—being hired by the Society to find Dyson.

Cornelius steepled his fingers. "We don't even know that there's a situation. He could have simply double-booked. For all we know, Dyson had brunch with a lady friend."

Ah. We'd already hit the negotiation phase. Not sure how I'd missed the whole front end of that conversation. Wait...lady friend?

I caught movement out of the corner of my eye and shifted quickly away from Alex in an attempt to save my shins. I also wiped all expression from my face and then focused on exuding an aura of polite interest.

"If you thought he was brunching with one of his women, you wouldn't have brought Celia in. She doesn't work for free." Alex leaned back in his chair and crossed an ankle over his knee.

Cornelius frowned. "She claims the cost of quality kibble has increased. As if she feeds that beast dog food. The hound found very little trace of him in the building, so he did not make it so far as headquarters this morning." He sighed. "All right, let's assume there's an actual problem. I need this to be your top priority."

Alex named a jaw-dropping sum. And then the negotiations began.

I stayed quiet as a mouse and tried not to interrupt, and eventually they came around to me.

"You'll want your baby vamp to assist, I assume?"

Alex nodded.

I would have to remember to thank him for the staunch support and bubbling enthusiasm that he showed.

To me, Cornelius said, "Same terms as last time."

It wasn't couched as an offer, but rather a done deal.

"No."

Cornelius leaned back in his chair. "Oh?"

"I want payment within thirty days." I'd missed that last time. "And my name is Mallory. Not baby vamp, not little anything. Mallory. Or Ms. Andrews." I narrowed my eyes in my best attempt at a Clint Eastwood stare.

And then I waited. So hard for me since the transformation. My impulse control wasn't the greatest these days. In fact, that might have been part of my problem with being hungry all the time. A little bit of hunger seemed to go a long way.

Cornelius stood up, and—my eyeballs almost bulged out of my skull—extended his hand. I didn't even know what to do. I'd forgotten to ask Alex or Wembley *why* the enhanced rarely shook hands. I shot Alex a covert glance. And he inclined his head very slightly.

I clasped Cornelius's hand and shook it firmly.

"A pleasure doing business with you, Ms. Andrews." A smile played about the corners of his mouth, but it never quite broke free.

I'd either passed a test or he was laughing at me. Did I really care which? I mentally shrugged, then stood up to follow Alex out into the hall.

After he'd closed the door behind me, I turned to Alex and cringed. "Does this mean I have to call him Mr. Lemann now?"

Alex grinned. "Not at all. I would say the opposite. Good job."

"You can say that. You're making enough to pay my downtown condo mortgage for a year, plus utilities, plus condo fees, plus the payment on my former fab sports car." I shook my head, surprised all over again at the large sum. "Is this a sexism thing?"

"It's a qualifications thing. As in, I'm qualified, and you're..." He considered me. "You're more an accessory."

If I didn't know he was intentionally pushing my buttons, I'd have nailed him in the nuts. My sword instructor and I had been working on increasing my comfort level with conflict and physical contact. Who would have thought I'd be so physically timid when I had basically no verbal filter?

But it looked like he was doing a good job. I'd have to tell him next time I saw him.

"Do you think Ms. Bland and Boring is still here? Reorganizing orientation, maybe?"

Alex blinked. "Who, Becky? She's not bland." He slowed down, giving Ms. Boring a second mental look. "She's kind of hot. Yeah." His pace picked back up.

"Really? I don't see it." I tried to conjure up a picture of her, but her image eluded me. All I had was the impression she'd left with me that morning: competent but bland. And bored with the work she was doing. "What is she?"

"A coyote."

That was the second time I'd heard of them, and it wasn't any clearer to me now what a coyote was.

"Since she's clearly two legged and human, and she's not a werecoyote—what exactly is she?" I'd already gotten a chuckle over werewolves, so I figured were-creatures weren't a thing.

"What the heck is a werecoyote supposed to be?" Alex opened the door to the retail shop.

I'd been in such a rush chasing Alex and Cornelius through the Employees Only door, and before that I'd had a dead body on my mind, and before that I'd been late to orientation and in a hurry... Wow, this day had been packed. But because of the various distractions, I hadn't paid any attention to the retail store displays. Which was a shame, because the public face of the Society was always entertaining.

I fell behind Alex and made my way in a much more leisurely fashion to the exterior door. "Oh, these are new!"

Three display stands held beautifully, elaborately constructed witch hats.

Alex had U-turned at the door and now stood at my

shoulder. "They're here on consignment. With Halloween just around the corner, the designer thought the chances of an on-site sale were good enough to risk taking these three off her website."

I ran my finger over the velvety material. "Can I try one on?"

Alex sighed. "Sure. We don't have anything else to do."

"Please. It'll take two seconds." As I fiddled with the pins attaching the hat to the stand, I realized the store was unmanned. "Where's the shopgirl?"

"She hightailed it when security told her they weren't sure how long the building would be shut down." Alex took the hat from me after a few failed attempts to settle it squarely on my head. "She's a good kid; she should be back soon."

He fiddled with it a bit, then, holding it in place, said, "Have a look."

I turned to the mirror behind the stand. "Wow. It's gorgeous. But I'd never get it to stay on."

"You have the hair for it. Just pile all that hair up on your head, and you can use a proper hatpin to stabilize it."

"And how do you know that?"

Alex gave me a funny look. "Women used to wear hats—every day. You do know that, right?" Then he grinned.

"What?"

"It's a *little* funny: the vamp with the witch hat."

"Like I'd try on the fake fangs. I have more self-respect than that." Or I'd already bought a pair on the sly because I was dying to try them on.

"Right."

I took off the hat and put it back on the stand. "If it's still here in a few days, I'll come back and pick it up."

"So much restraint. How unlike you."

"Yeah, I've been working a little on that. I try to restrain myself, unless I feel compelled—just in case Wembley is right, and I do have a touch of precognition. You never know."

Alex refrained from calling Wembley a complete joker for believing in precognition enhancements, but he looked skeptical as he unlocked the front door and let me out of the shop.

"You'd think the fact that my progenitor could read minds—"

"In close proximity."

"Okay," I said. "Close proximity or not, still reading minds. You really think precog is that far removed?"

"Without question. I'm driving," he said. When I started to get my keys out, Alex said, "No, let's take mine."

I didn't see his Accord anywhere in the lot. Then he clicked the car's remote entry fob, and the lights flashed on a Nissan Juke.

"New car?" I asked, though it looked like it was a few years old. "Or new to you?"

"Sort of. I own a used car dealership." He rolled his eyes when he saw the look on my face. "A very small one. It's convenient for the Society to have access to a place where they can dump cars and pick up new ones."

"You do know that sounds incredibly shady."

He shrugged. "It is shady. Not the transactions, but the reasons for rotating cars. We live in a secret society. In case you've forgotten."

"Yeah, I know. I can't really forget, not when someone like you will come and chop my head off if I let the big secret out."

He pulled out of the parking lot. "Of course not. We're a

just society. We'll bring you in to be hanged after a very brief judicial hearing."

I groaned. I knew he was right, but to be so flip...

"So about you and Wembley—"

"Wait a sec," I said. "Where are we going? I have a date at two."

"A date?" He cocked his head, but didn't take his eyes off the road. "With who?

"Bradley. He doesn't handle change well, and he used to meet with Mrs. A once a week at two p.m. for tea and cookies. Nuts. I need to pick up shortbread." I shook my head. "Yeah, yeah. I know I can't eat it, but Bradley likes shortbread."

"And you abstain because...?"

"I'm dieting." I fluttered my lashes at him.

"That's rich." Alex pulled onto the westbound highway. "It works out well that we're only going out to Gladys's house for a quick check-in. I want to make sure the calm we witnessed this morning wasn't shock, and she's still holding it together. The last thing we need is her falling apart at an inconvenient moment."

It seemed like a waste of time, since we'd practically just come from there. Then I thought about it...Gladys, dead man, her bedroom, her nice sheets, the herb garden... "Yeah, good choice. In and out, then I'm off to Bradley's...and then—Becky?"

"Yeah. I'll call and make an appointment with her after your tea with Bradley, assuming she'll be available. How long does this bizarre ritual usually take?"

"It is not a bizarre ritual. It's a comforting, regularly scheduled event that both Bradley and I enjoy." I waited briefly for an apology then figured I must be smoking something to think that might happen. "Usually about an hour, so schedule at four to give us a little squish room."

Then I stewed a bit. I was a little surprised I hadn't thought to set up a follow-up appointment with Gladys myself. I'd just accepted her calm at face value.

After the silence had stretched out to several minutes, Alex said, "After I schedule with Becky, I'll see if I can get in touch with Rachael."

I nodded. "Sorry—I'm just really annoyed about forgetting the shortbread and taking Gladys at face value. What is up with me today?"

"Roses and witch hats?"

"Yeah." I sighed. "I'm working on it. I swear I went from a steel-trap brain to a sieve."

I really was working on it—but slowly. Because I wasn't about to give up the ability to stop and enjoy life as it happened, including the roses and witch hats. Improve my filter? Sure. Increase my impulse control? Yep. Go back to being a hyper-scheduled, anxiety-ridden, miserable person? Well, not miserable, but not-super-happy person? No way.

"Uh-huh. Do you have a calendar on your phone?" he asked. I replied in the affirmative, and he said, "Use it. For everything. And you can even set reminders that make an annoying ding noise."

I was about to say "brilliant" in a snarky tone, but I stopped because—while not brilliant—it was a reasonable and rather obvious solution. Why wasn't I already using my phone? I used to use much more sophisticated scheduling software at work. Perhaps because I considered myself on vacation, or worse, permanently unemployed—so the thought had simply never occurred.

It hit me like a flash. "This is basically my job now."

"What is?"

"This." I flicked my finger between the two of us. "Being a vamp. And afterlife coaching. My life is basically my job now, whereas my job was my life before."

"This way sounds better to me."

I grinned at him. "Me too. And I think I can schedule my life without worrying about having an anxiety attack."

"Probably so." He looked at me oddly. But he couldn't see it, because he hadn't known me before. "Are you planning on buying a place anytime soon? I thought living with Wembley was a temporary fix."

"I was going to buy one of his rehabbed flip houses, but I thought it was in the same neighborhood as his current project. Turns out he thought I'd love this other house because it *wasn't* in the same neighborhood." I shrugged. "Southwest, not far from Gladys. Do I look like a southwest Austin vampire to you?"

"I'm thinking you think there's a right and wrong answer to that question, so I'm going with silence."

I frowned at him. "I'm a southeast Austin vampire."

"I have no idea what that means."

"Only because you don't get intuition. I feel at home in Wembley's neighborhood. And I like his current house. It feels right—hence, my intuition must be speaking to me." I wiggled excitedly in my seat, doing the seated version of a happy dance. "I've already given him an offer, but conditional upon him staying and finishing the house."

Something between a groan and a laugh emanated from Alex's chest. "I vaguely remember telling you that Wembley wasn't exactly mentor material."

I did have a vague recollection of that. "Okay. But he's not my mentor; he's my roommate and my friend."

"Just file away the fact that Wembley isn't like other vamps. He's lost an edge that most have."

I felt like I was missing something, but I was also pretty sure if I pushed for more information that I'd get the wall of silence. No, the wall of vagueness.

I took out my phone and started entering appointments. I lifted the phone. "See, I can change. Making appointments right now. Where will we meet Becky? She doesn't have an office at headquarters, does she?"

"No, she's always worked with Dyson out of his home office."

"Whoa—what?" I tapped save and put my phone aside. This was big news. "You guys said they'd worked together for a while now, but she worked *at his house*? They must have been tight. What did she do for him?"

"Odds and ends. Officially she was his assistant, but I think she'd do just about anything for him."

"Hm, well, I'm guessing we should meet at headquarters. It seems awkward to interview the assistant at the wife's house." I did some mental logistics. "The wife doesn't know she's a widow, and technically we need to interview her about her husband's disappearance...but it still seems wrong to show up at the house of a woman who is an unknowing widow. I'm divided. She's definitely a prime suspect. And Becky, too, because she sounds basically like Dyson's work wife. Ooooh. Maybe there was tension between Becky and Mrs. Dyson." I nodded when the facts lined up. "Clearly we need to interview Becky at headquarters, because we want her alone. Maybe Mrs. Dyson and Becky will give us dirt on each other if we interview them separately."

"Slow down and let the facts catch up. We have no idea what the situation at Dyson's is like. And no one is a suspect, because we have no information." He shifted in his seat.

"But let's say we did have a suspect list—remember that there's a kid, too. Rachael Dyson."

I considered the concept of golems and kids, and...no. Just no. "Since we're on suspects, what about political enemies? Dyson must have run the Society—sort of. I mean, Cornelius seems to actually be around more than this guy was, but—"

"No, Dyson ran the Society. The man was a workhorse. He had his finger in every pie." Alex pulled into Gladys's driveway. He turned to me and said, "Let's keep this low key. In and out, as long as Gladys looks like she's got everything under control."

"And if she doesn't?" I narrowed my eyes at him. "Where's your sword?"

"Always with me. And no, I will not lop off her head. Give me a break; we're trying to prevent an unjust hanging, remember?"

Before I could reply, a car pulled into the drive next to Alex's Juke.

A very attractive, fit blonde woman in a sleeveless A-line dress stepped out of a sporty Mercedes. She fluttered her beautifully manicured fingers at us and waited for us to get out of the car.

My stomach fluttered, and I wasn't sure if that was my intuition acting up or just hunger pangs.

"Go on. See what the lovely lady wants," Alex said right before he rolled my window down for me.

I pasted what had to be a patently false bright smile on my face. "Hi! How are you doing?"

"Just fabulous. Divorced three months and loving it. I'm Lyndsay. Are you here for the Divorced Divas party too?" She shot Alex a curious look.

It had definitely been my intuition twitching and not my

stomach. Well, maybe both, because my stomach was always pretty pushy. I took a breath and said, "Absolutely." I waved a dismissive hand in Alex's direction. "Our date ran just a little long. But I told him I couldn't miss this party."

Lyndsay's eyes were bulging out of her head. She stage-whispered to me, "Now that's some stamina—all night and well into the morning. You go, girl." And then she fist-bumped me. With the exploding hand and everything. Not what I would have expected from the high-heeled, well-groomed, Southern-drawling woman in front of me.

I got out of the car and closed the door, then leaned in through the window to find a vastly amused Alex grinning back at me. "Feel free to pass my number out."

I wrinkled my nose at him. "I will not. Pick me up in half an hour?"

"Done."

He drove off without a backward glance, leaving me with a gaggle of divorced divas, and who knew what kind of party.

5

YOGA YIELDS RESULTS

Turned out, the party had nothing at all to do with sex toys, which had been my first suspicion.

No, it was much worse. It was a garden party. And all I could think about was dead guy under the herbs. It was like a mantra playing over and over in my head. *Dead guy under the herbs. Dead guy under the herbs.*

They'd say, "So nice to meet you." And I'd have to bite my tongue not to say, "Dead guy under the herbs."

Talk about working on my filter.

Gladys had been surrounded by a pack of dazzling women from the moment I'd arrived, so I hadn't been able to ask her how she was coping. All signs, however, pointed to quite well.

She finally lost her entourage, so I grabbed the moment and hurried to her side. "What were you thinking?"

"You think too soon?" Gladys gazed over each of the clustered groups of women: all under fifty, all fashionable, all divorced. "It's been two months since the divorce was finalized. I almost feel like I waited too long. As soon as I signed the papers, I wanted to throw a big bash."

"About the herb garden, I mean."

"Ah. That the bed was bare, and I'd been planning to plant an herb garden there for weeks. Why?"

Why? Why?

"Well, you have evidence of a crime in your yard. And people are everywhere, tromping around within feet of a dead body." I was getting really good at covert conversations, but this one... I lowered my voice yet more. "A dead body under the herbs...the same herbs that they're putting in their mojitos."

In a very reasonable tone, she said, "They don't know that. Besides, it's not like he's done much decomposing down there."

Okay, both of those statements were actually true. And Gladys was more than cool under fire. She behaved as if there were no fire. Uh-oh. I might be the problem child in this scenario.

She let out a little sigh. "I could hardly cancel, could I? What reason would I give? We've all been so excited about starting this club. Why are you here again? You're not divorced." She arched her perfect auburn eyebrows. "Are you?"

"No. Never married."

She leaned down and kissed my cheek. "Smart girl. Now, I think that's your ride come to pick you up. Quickly, before someone latches on to Alex and takes him home—what did you need from me?"

"Just to make sure you're doing okay..." She gave me a reassuring smile, and I continued. "And to see if you'd thought of anything else, now that, you know...you've had a little time to process everything."

"I do have something." She held up a finger. "Just a minute." And then disappeared into the house.

Alex was turning down propositions left and right and slowly making his way to me. When he arrived, he had a cat-in-cream look on his face.

"Oh, please. It's bad enough I have to watch it happen. Don't smirk."

"Honestly, I don't usually find it this entertaining—but watching you get annoyed makes the experience more than a little amusing." He turned to the house. "So how's Gladys?"

"Fine. Completely, not-a-hair-out-of-place fine." A rather unpleasant thought surfaced. "You don't think she's actually capable... There's no way..."

He hesitated just a beat then said, "No. I don't think she had anything to do with his death. For whatever reason, the killer thought Gladys was the perfect fall guy. Or the perfect stash spot. Here she comes. And she's waving a piece of paper at us."

When she arrived, she looked quite pleased with herself. "I meditated this morning after you left, and this is what I came up with. I hope it's helpful."

Alex snatched the folded piece of paper before I could—that wizardly speed and dexterity at play.

"Thank you, Gladys," I said, though I hadn't a clue what meditation had to do with anything. "And sorry for gate-crashing. The wine was lovely, and dead body notwithstanding, your garden is gorgeous."

I'd been terrified to try any of the cocktails for fear of some herby addition, like in the mojitos.

"I'm glad you dropped by." She arched an eyebrow. "Even if you've never been divorced."

"We'll be swinging by this evening again," Alex said.

He must have checked with his body-stashing source. I

had to swallow the laughter burbling up in my throat. Body-stashing...a small snicker escaped. I coughed.

But Gladys just inclined her head politely. "You're more than welcome—but why?"

Excellent question, Gladys. I turned to see what Alex's response would be: truth or fiction.

"We need to remove the body in case the killer decides to point the finger at you. And I have someone who can do an autopsy on the sly."

And I thought unfettered access to a used car dealership was shady. Now he had a medical examiner on the payroll?

"No problem," Gladys replied. "When's good for you? I'm open all evening."

Gladys was a wonder. She truly was.

"Midnight?" Alex asked.

She nodded. "Till then. Toodles." And she headed off to chat with a small group of tittering women who clearly had their eyes on Alex.

In the driveway, Alex opened the folded piece of paper. "Clever, clever lady."

"What?"

He handed the paper to me. In it was a detailed account of Gladys's movements from late afternoon until the next morning.

"What does this have to do with meditation?" I asked.

Alex shrugged then opened the driver's door. Once inside, he waited for me to take a seat and then said, "Maybe it clears her head, makes her focus sharper. Who knows? Wait, didn't you tell her to take yoga and consider meditation to help with relaxation?"

"Well, yes. I read that they both help—I haven't actually practiced either of them. Do I look like I need help relaxing and embracing my inner light?"

Alex inhaled a sharp breath. "That's a terrifying thought—you embracing your inner light any more than you already do."

I rolled my eyes. Then I caught sight of the time. "You're going to have to take me to Bradley's. You can drop me off at the mini-grocery on the corner. They carry his favorite shortbread."

"Check the bag."

"What—" Then I saw the small cloth bag at my feet. *That* bag.

I opened it to find two popular brands of shortbread, one of which was Bradley's brand. "You went to the grocery store?"

"It was that or hang out in the driveway, lurking like a creepy stalker as all the guests arrived."

"I don't think they'd have minded you lurking one bit—but thank you. Bradley really doesn't like change, and tardiness makes him nervous."

I glanced at Alex. He really was a decent guy—minus the creepy spirits that stalked him and whispered evil nothings in his ear. And his incredibly annoying way of attracting any woman within a thirty-foot radius. And then there was the question of his age...

"You'll have to introduce me sometime," Alex said.

"Sure," I mumbled without thinking. "Oh. Maybe. Bradley's a little funny with strangers. How old exactly are you?"

Alex raised an eyebrow and glanced at me. "Does it matter?"

"Why are you so secretive about it?"

"Times change, people change. The past is in the past. And dwelling on numbers, on age, is a way to reflect on that passing time." His face hardened. "No thanks."

"Oh. I didn't realize it was a sensitive subject. So don't ask Wembley how old he is?"

Alex's head tilted and his features softened. "I'm surprised it hasn't come up, given Tangwystl."

"What does my sword have to do with anything?"

"Tangwystl and Wembley have a long history. She's made her way back to him a few times, and he's found her a few different partners. Speaking of, you shouldn't leave her at home."

"She's hard to tote around, and I still don't have a clue how to use a sword." I massaged my hand, still a little sore from sword practice with my instructor a few days ago. "But having been in a dangerous situation with a fantastic weapon and no clue how to use it does motivate a girl." I tilted my head. "Maybe not as motivating as cinnamon-spiked coffee and spicy, high-sodium vegetable juice combined."

"That's disgusting," Alex said, then scowled. "I told you I'd help. And even Wembley, out of practice as he is, could teach you a thing or two."

After my encounter with my evil, murdering progenitor, I figured I had a few options. Risk death due to ignorance, or hit up one of several sword-wielding members of the Society. I'd thumbed my nose at both options—hence Alex's annoyance—and started lessons with a local human guy who knew a lot about swords and fighting. He also happened to be easy on the eyes and incredibly nice. So I'd scored on all counts.

"You know, I do remember Wembley saying he was going to start training again. So I guess he was into swords at some point?"

"You could say that. Ask him to tell you some pillaging stories someday."

"Right." Pillaging did not sound like a subject I'd enjoying hearing about. "Wait a minute—do you know why Tangwystl has had so many partners?"

I'd gotten a vague explanation that her former partners hadn't been vamps, from which I'd assumed they'd not lived supernaturally long lives. But maybe there was some other reason.

Alex shifted his grip on the wheel. "Learn how to use a sword, carry her now so you can accustom yourself, and keep practicing. Always keep practicing."

"Ohmygod—they were slaughtered, weren't they?" I tipped my head down and closed my eyes as I considered how long the line of prematurely dead people who'd carried Tangwystl might be. I clutched my shortbread close against my stomach. "I knew there was a catch."

"They're dead, yes. Otherwise you wouldn't have the sword. And people aren't as long-lived as magic swords, especially the living kind. But the only 'catch' that Tangwystl has is free will." Alex sounded disgusted with the idea.

I put aside his weird issue with my sword's absolutely adorable—though somewhat violent—personality and tried to do the math. Why would a living sword last longer than a not-living magic sword? And if living swords lived extra-long sword lives and Wembley had been hooked up with Tangwystl for a long time now... "How old is Wembley?" Alex remained silent. Annoyingly, unhelpfully silent. "Okay, fine. How is it that Wembley's still around to find more partners for Tangwystl and yet those partners are dropping like flies?"

"It's hardly like that. Some of Tangwystl's partners have been normal humans. Some were reckless. Some lived a very long time. Wembley's just lived longer. He's a survivor."

"But not a good mentor?" I asked, because I couldn't

resist. I'd love to know what Alex's hang-up with Wembley was.

"Not in his current state."

Alex liked Wembley, but he didn't typically like vamps. And yet Wembley wasn't a good mentor. What was the deal between the two of them? I let the silence linger as long as I could, but Alex didn't drop any additional nuggets about Wembley.

When we were almost at my condo building, I said, "I'll bring the sword tonight."

"Good plan. And just a heads-up: I'm planning to ask Wembley to join us. We might need some extra hands."

"Sounds good." I grabbed my purse and the bag of shortbread. "Thanks again for the shortbread. It was thoughtful of you."

He smiled, but it had a grim tinge. "See you in an hour."

"Perfect." I slammed the Juke's door.

Bradley buzzed me in at exactly three minutes to two, making my timely arrival likely. Bradley should be happy.

As I made my way up to his condo on the fourth floor, I realized it was the third visit I'd made since we started the weekly tea appointment. I'd be passing by my now-rented condo, on the same floor as Bradley's, and also by Mrs. A's place.

I missed her. She'd been my neighbor, a little too nosy, a little too brash—but one of the few people who had bothered to get to know me before my transformation, when I was perhaps a less pleasant person to know. And for that kindness, she'd been killed. Not exactly, but close enough. She'd been about her normal nosy routine, keeping an eye on the comings and goings of neighbors and their visitors, when she'd seen a little too much. That was why she'd really been killed.

But it was all tied up together in my head. My transformation, her kindness, my progenitor killing her. So I had guilt, and I missed her.

I felt my throat burn. Crying wouldn't do. Not when I cried acid tears that burned my face. Stupid vampire tears. Only, vamps didn't cry. I cried and I was a vamp—but I stood all alone in that capacity. The crying vampire. Good grief, that could *never* get out. What a terrible nickname.

I juggled my purse and the grocery bag so I could take out the special cloth hanky I'd started carrying. Then I dabbed at my eyes and knocked on Bradley's door.

When Bradley opened the door, I leaned in to hug him, and he tolerated it. He wasn't a big fan of physical contact, but I was of the theory that if he practiced with someone he liked, it would get better. I assumed, of course, that Bradley actually liked me. He'd never indicated otherwise, so I was sticking to that assumption.

"Have you been crying?" he asked.

I stepped back, surprised. "Why do you ask?"

"Your eyes get really red and you smell like garlic when you cry."

"Really?" I cried acid tears that smelled like garlic. Ugh. That was just weird. And why hadn't anyone mentioned it before? Why couldn't *I* smell the garlic?

"Yes. Mrs. A said that commenting on personal attributes is rude. Unless it's a compliment. Is that a compliment for a vampire?"

I stood in his doorway and stared at him in stunned silence. I'd *never* told Bradley I was a vampire. Wouldn't have dreamed of it. Couldn't have imagined doing it.

Bad. Very bad.

6

CRIME-FIGHTING VAMP

"Come in." When I didn't move, Bradley said, "I can't close the door."

I stepped into his condo. "Sorry."

He closed the door and then abandoned me for his tea preparations. I could hear the soft whistling of the kettle as it reached the boiling point.

My brain was screaming, "Deny!" But I couldn't say the words. I walked slowly into the kitchen, where the teacups and small plates were set out.

Bradley retrieved the tiny plate we used for cookies from the place setting where I usually sat. "You don't need this."

"I think I'm supposed to say something like: vampires aren't real."

Bradley looked up from the stove where he was retrieving the kettle of boiled water. "I don't understand."

I squished up my face. What to say? Definitely the truth, but which truth? "It's supposed to be a secret."

"I'm good at keeping secrets. I know all sorts of stuff about Mrs. A." He stopped, considered, then said, "I can't tell you. They're secrets."

"I bet you're fabulous at keeping secrets." I sighed. "It's not very safe to know these particular secrets. At least, I don't think so."

He seemed to consider my answer and then simply walked away. He headed straight for the teapot on the table and filled it with boiling water. After he'd returned the kettle to the stove, he came back and asked, "Would you like to have a seat?"

"Yes, thank you." I sat down in my designated spot.

This was our ritual, and it had to be a good sign that he was following it.

Once he was sitting down, he checked the timer. But there were still a few minutes left. He clasped his hands loosely in his lap. "Did a vampire kill Mrs. A?"

I felt my eyes burn again.

Bradley pulled out a startlingly white cotton handkerchief and handed it to me. "I miss her too."

Dabbing at my eyes, I said, "I bet you do."

The hanky he'd handed me had his initials embroidered in the corners: BC for Bradley Carson. The stitching wasn't perfect; it was clearly homemade. And I knew immediately that the only person in Bradley's life who'd have cared enough to embroider hankies for him was Mrs. A.

And I bawled.

I did my best to soak up the tears before they streaked my face with red marks. It wasn't just Mrs. A. It was also the relief of someone from my previous life knowing about my vamp-hood, no matter how tenuous our previous connection. I hadn't realized how much the secret had weighed on me—not until now.

Bradley sat across from me, looking awkwardly away.

"Sorry," I said from behind the hanky. At least I didn't get a runny nose. I couldn't imagine how bad vampire snot would be.

"Did a vampire kill her?"

"Yes. The same one who bit me." Wadding up the hanky in my hand, I asked, "How did you know? About me being a vampire."

"You never eat. You had those fang marks on your lip. And your roommate is a vampire."

"Ah." I looked at Bradley with new respect. The guy managed to get through life mostly avoiding people, he rarely left his condo, and yet he'd come up with the scoop on my super-secret underground community. "And how do you know about Wembley?"

"That's not his name."

"I'm sorry—what?"

"That's not his real name." He pulled out his phone and opened an app. With a few taps and a swipe, he pulled up the relevant screen then slid the phone across the table to me.

On the screen was a photograph of a very detailed sketch. And it resembled Wembley, but it wasn't the Wembley I knew. Sharpen up the squishy edges, un-hippify his beard, add a lot of muscle weight—a lot—and a massive sword. Oh, and this guy, he went by the name Einarr. "Einarr?"

"Army of one. Or maybe undead warrior. There are differing opinions."

I knew which one I voted for. I shook my head. Oh, Wembley. "And where did you get this?"

"It's an app I created. Confidentially. But the last two payments didn't come through, so the anonymous client is in breach of contract." He poured both of us tea. "That means I don't have to keep it confidential."

"Oh, no. No, no. You cannot tell anyone about this." Visions of Bradley with his head chopped off or hanged flashed before her eyes. "This is bad, Bradley. Do you know who your client was?"

"Anonymous. It means that I don't know his or her identity. That's the definition of anonymous."

"Right." I looked at the picture. It was almost like a playing card. EINARR was at the top, but there was more information below in a smaller type. I tried to blow up the picture but couldn't.

"Swipe left to turn the page for the player's stats."

The player? But I swiped. Aliases: Jefferson Wembley, Konrad Schwartz, Leopold Durtz, Mathias Larsen... There were at least a dozen listed. Enhancement: Vampire, class 3.

"What does 'class three' mean?" I asked.

"I don't know."

I swiped left again, but nothing happened.

"Some of the players only have one page of stats. You can tap the menu button to search for other players." He sipped his tea. "You're not in the app. You weren't in the source materials."

This was a nightmare. What would Alex say? Worse, what would Cornelius do? Specifically to poor Bradley, who had an encyclopedia of enhanced humans. A complete and utter nightmare.

"You do understand that these aren't players in a game?"

"I do now. After you changed, then you told me you caught Mrs. A's killer but it wasn't in the news, and then meeting your roommate. All the pieces fit."

"I see." But I didn't. Not at all. How he'd taken the little bits and pieces of information and woven them together to recreate a hidden truth—no, I didn't really see. "You said you have source materials for this app? What were they? An email, a shared file, access to some database?"

"A handwritten book."

"Like a journal?"

"No. Like a handwritten book. Your tea is getting cold."

Clearly, Bradley was not feeling the urgency and concern that I was. But I drank some tea, because it would make him happy.

"You forgot the milk."

"Actually, now that the cat's out of the bag about my vampire secret—milk doesn't really agree with me." I wrinkled my nose and gave him an apologetic smile. "Does anyone else have access to the app besides you?"

"The client. I provided regular updates in accordance with the contract. This one is complete, but the version the client has is ninety-two percent complete."

I bit my lip. "No one else?"

"I can't answer that question. I have no control over the client's actions."

"Right." Images of the app going viral filled my head. "I need to talk to my friend Alex about this. I have serious concerns for your safety."

"If you tell him, more people will know. Did you bring shortbread?"

I'd completely forgotten about it. I'd dropped the bag and my purse when I'd walked in and been confronted with Bradley's startling knowledge of my vampire-ness. "Sorry—let me just grab those."

I retrieved the bag, pulled out his favorites and handed them over for our tea, and stashed the others in his cupboard for later.

When I sat back down, he was patiently waiting for me

before he helped himself to the cookies. He tried really hard to stick to the rules that Mrs. A had shared with him, because they gave him a way to interact with other people that he could understand and that made people more predictable. He'd told me that the visit before last.

We spent several minutes talking about the weather—always hot in September in Austin, even late September—and Mrs. A's funeral—gorgeous, because Bradley had followed her wishes to the letter. Say what you like about Mrs. A's stitchery and her cooking, her taste was exceptional.

"Oh, the funeral. I'd forgotten you met Wembley there."

Bradley nodded. "I returned the handwritten book. The client treated it as though it were valuable, but he didn't have the right equipment to create high-resolution pictures from the illustrations."

"Do you think your client was a man?"

"I don't know. Maybe." He frowned. "Are you a crime-fighting vampire?"

I bit back a grin. The way he said it, he made me sound like a superhero. "Not usually. But..." I shouldn't. I crossed my arms. I really shouldn't. But he already knew about vampires—and who knew what else was in that app? I leaned forward. "But there *is* something I'm working on now."

Bradley smiled.

It almost made me cry again. Bradley never smiled.

"Can I help?"

No, of course not. Becoming even more involved in the enhanced community, on the Society's radar...bad idea. But crushing that tiny bit of potential happiness, the hint of blooming joy...impossible.

"There's a murder—we think, but we won't have an

autopsy until tonight—and the body's buried under this new vampire's herb garden, and..."

His smile grew as I told him all of the juicy details. It took me about ten minutes to update him.

"So you have a list of suspects?" he asked.

"We do. There's the wife and the daughter, because they probably had the opportunity and a likely financial motive —still checking up on that. And the assistant, because she worked in really close quarters with him and likely had opportunity. And then his political enemies, because they had motive but no clue about opportunity."

"Do you want to know what's in the will?"

"Definitely. Can you find that?"

"Once it's been filed in probate court, I can."

"No, that hasn't happened yet. No one but Alex and I know he's dead, so definitely not."

"But then there's no financial motive. For the will to be executed, your victim has to be found."

I knocked on the table. "I knew I forgot something important. That's one of the reasons we're retrieving the body tonight. For the autopsy, but also so Gladys—that's the lady who found Dyson—isn't implicated. If the murderer wants Dyson found, then they'll have to point the Society at Gladys."

"It's hard to verify the family's motive without the will. If you write the full names of your suspects down, I can look for clues in their backgrounds." When I blinked at him in astonishment, he said, "Online."

As if I'd imagined him leaving his condo. I should have said no. I really should have. But my very own sidekick was too much to resist.

I stuck my hand out.

He didn't even stop to think about it. While he pumped my hand enthusiastically, I said, "And I promise not to ever call you an accessory."

Bradley blinked at me owlishly. "I don't know what that means, but okay."

7

VEGGIE JUICE BRIBES

Alex picked me up at the curb. All it took was one look, and he was on to me.

"What happened?"

The man had a suspicious nature...perhaps amplified by his experience with me. But I wasn't the root cause, because that suspicious, edgy part of his personality went much deeper than a few-weeks-long acquaintanceship could produce.

I opened my eyes wide. But I didn't go so far as to *deny* that anything had happened.

"Don't even try. Your eyes are red and there's just a hint of garlic in the air. You've obviously been crying."

How was it I was the only person who didn't know I smelled like an Italian restaurant every time I got a little teary? I contemplated the few times I'd cried. There really weren't that many. It wasn't like I cried at the drop of a hat. An especially commendable quality, since transformation was a trying time when one's progenitor was a homicidal maniac.

"And you look guilty as sin," he said.

"I have a few updates." I gave him a squinty-eyed look. "Although you really could have told me I smell like spaghetti when I get a little teary."

"A lot teary. It's not really noticeable unless you really let loose. But whatever is in those poisonous tears of yours, it irritates your eyes no matter how little you produce."

I flipped open the vanity mirror, and, sure enough, I looked like I had pink eye. Nice.

"It doesn't last that long. Probably back to normal in an hour or so." Alex sighed. "Spit it out. Other than having an emotional reunion with Bradley, what happened?"

I really, really didn't want to tell him. Because it would be bad. And I wasn't sure which part was worse. The unintentional reveal of the entirety of the Society's membership rolls, the existence of the app in unknown hands, or my solicitation of Bradley's help, i.e. the recruitment of my very own personal sidekick.

He reached behind his seat at a stop light and pulled out a bottle of spicy veggie juice.

I grabbed but he held it against his chest, inaccessible. "It's not cold."

"Don't care."

"I give you the juice, if you give me the information."

"Withholding food from a starving woman? You would really do that?" I gave him a nasty look.

"In no century are you scary, so don't try. And the only reason you're starving is because you don't plan well." He wiggled the juice at me.

My stomach protested. "Not like I wasn't going to tell you. I can't believe you're bribing me with veggie juice."

"Spicy veggie juice."

I snatched the bottle from him. "Bradley made an app for a board game that lists all of the game's players, except they're all Society members." I popped the top and chugged most of the small bottle, but I kept half an eye on Alex.

"His project or a freelance gig?"

I squinted at him. He was taking this much better than I'd predicted. "Freelance. The information came from an old handwritten book that he returned to the anonymous client. Did you know Wembley's real name is Einarr?"

And then I saw the white-knuckled grip he had on the steering wheel. Uh-oh.

"I did, but it's hardly common knowledge."

"Huh." My eyeballs wouldn't budge from the steering wheel. It really looked like he wanted to wring someone's neck. Maybe mine.

"Be careful if you mention Einarr to Wembley. That was a long time ago, and he was a different person." He still sounded relaxed, in spite of the wringing the steering wheel was getting. It was a little creepy. "Any clue what happened with the client or who he was?" Alex asked in that unnaturally calm voice.

"Um, do you want me to drive? You're making me a little nervous."

That seemed to surprise him. He glanced at me and then relaxed. "Not as nervous as I'll be with you driving."

That sounded a little more like the guy I knew, and his hands had relaxed on the wheel. I sank back in my seat. "The client is AWOL. Disappeared before making the last two payments, but he did get an early version of the app. And Bradley never knew who he was. He was a paranoid security nut. He thought the world was after his awesome game idea."

"He was probably right—just not the *human* world." He sighed. "I need to update Cornelius right away."

"There's a little more."

"A little?"

"A very small thing. Maybe don't tell Cornelius this one." I watched as Alex's lips thinned. I told him the rest before he could say something truly unpleasant. "I told Bradley about the murder, and now he's helping us."

"Good Lord." He gave me a narrow-eyed, very peeved look. "If we weren't on a such a tight schedule, we'd be headed back to Bradley's condo and I would be having a chat with him."

"I'm new to being a vampire and my verbal filter isn't what it could be—but I'm still an adult, making adult choices. Bradley already knew about us; I did not break some sacred trust. And he is very trustworthy. Very. And stable. And not even a little moody. Or broody."

"I'm neither moody nor broody. And if you think I am, consider that you might be particularly aggravating."

"One hundred percent talking about Bradley right now."

"Uh-huh. How is your friendly shut-in planning to help?"

"He's going to pull up background on the suspects and dig through them for clues." Since I wasn't sure what he could possibly find, I left it at that. "But he won't be leaving his condo. He's very uncomfortable with people."

"Since Bradley is the same guy who created an app containing highly classified information that could now be on hundreds, thousands, potentially millions of phones across the world, the fact that he doesn't leave his condo doesn't exactly limit his ability to do harm, does it?"

I sank in my seat. That was a good point.

Alex pulled off the freeway at the headquarters exit. That was also the exit for my place—so I could still pretend that he was dropping me off at home.

"I don't suppose I could just slip away, go do some solo sleuthing, and let you chat with Cornelius?"

Alex looked at me like I was deranged. "No. You want to get paid, you come with me. Besides, it may not be so bad: maybe the Society is already aware."

From the grim set of his jaw, I'd guess he didn't believe that.

After he pulled into the parking lot, I said, "Let's do this."

But Alex had already gotten out of the car. I was the one sitting in the passenger seat, needing a motivational shove out the door. "I can do this," I whispered, and got out of the car.

Turned out Alex's optimistic hypothesis that the Society knew of the threat was complete fantasy.

I quaked in my seat as Cornelius's eyes quite literally shone icy blue.

Were those laser beams? Was I about to be diced into little pieces by terrifying assassin eyes? I didn't want to die that way. What was I thinking? I didn't want to die *period*.

"How did this happen? How?" he asked, his chilly, glowing eyes turning even lighter. They'd become a dense silvery color. If my eyes bled red, then Cornelius's bled silver. But if his eyes were bleeding...that meant he was losing control.

I glanced at the door.

"You're not anywhere near fast enough, Ms. Andrews."

Ooooh, was I regretting that name switch thing. "Ms. Andrews" really worked in his favor. It came out with a biting precision that made me flinch.

I trained my gaze on a point just over his left shoulder. I could still see his icy eyeballs from the corner of my eye, but it wasn't quite as terrifying.

"If your friend has created the worst reveal scandal of

the century before the century has barely begun, there will be consequences."

It almost would be better if he'd said what the consequences would be. I'd sit around for days conjuring up possible punishments for me and for poor Bradley. Then it occurred to me, what were the chances?

"Spit it out." Cornelius's voice was just as chilly as his eyes had been. "Now, Ms. Andrews!"

"I'm not sure if it's relevant..." I made the mistake of looking at Cornelius. His eyes looked like liquid mercury, not glowing anymore but creepier than a screeching black cat on Halloween in a graveyard. I swallowed. "Isn't it strange that Bradley, who lives in my building, ended up with the job creating an app containing an encyclopedia of the local enhanced community?"

"Not particularly." At least Cornelius's tone had downgraded from icily cutting to flat.

"Austin is the hub of enhanced living in Texas," Alex said. "And Bradley has an exceptional reputation in his field. It's a coincidence, but not as unusual as you'd think."

I glanced his way for the first time since Cornelius had gone all freaky-eyed. He didn't look particularly concerned about his boss. Distinctly unhappy, but not worried about the glacial eyeball display.

"Huh. So—what are you going to do?" I asked, even though I was scared to know. "Bradley is completely trustworthy. He doesn't want to hurt me or us or anything like that."

"Your attestation is duly recorded." Cornelius made a note on his computer. "Anton will be informed."

What had just happened? And why was the really scary version of Mr. Clean being informed of anything? "What's Anton got to do with my friend?"

Alex sighed. "Cornelius entered the information in our emergency response system. On the computer? The notes he's been taking? Anton's on call, so he's retrieving the app as we speak, and having a conversation with Bradley about how he needs to not disseminate information concerning the Society."

"Ohmygod—you cannot chop off Bradley's head." My heart thudded at a frantic rate. "He is a really good guy. Really. Awesome guy. Totally harmless."

My gaze darted between Alex and Cornelius. I hoped one of them would listen.

"Calm down," Alex said. "Bradley's fine. As long as he cooperates with Anton."

Cornelius's landline rang. When he answered, he sounded completely composed. "Yes?" But then a low rumble erupted from his chest and the icy, silvery eyes came back. "One moment. Let me pass the phone to Ms. Andrews."

Uh-oh. I leaned forward and took the phone from him, careful not to brush fingers...just in case he could freeze my digits.

"Hello?"

"Mallory, there's a man here who says I have to promise not to tell anyone about the Society. And sign paperwork. But I don't know him. And he won't let my attorney look at the papers."

I never thought I'd be so glad to hear Bradley's voice. And who knew Bradley had an attorney?

"Hey, Bradley. That's probably Anton. Big guy, lots of muscles, no hair, doesn't talk a lot. That the guy?"

"That is an accurate description."

"I know him, Bradley. And even though your attorney is bound by standards of professional conduct not to discuss your business, it really is best to keep this one just between you and the Society."

"I don't sign contracts before my attorney reviews them. Those are the rules."

I shifted the phone away from my face and covered it with my hand. "Do you have a copy of what you're asking him to sign?"

Cornelius tapped a few keys and then turned the monitor around.

I scanned the document and let out a sigh of relief. It really wasn't complicated. Speaking into the phone again, I said, "I just had a look at it, Bradley. It's fine. You're promising not talk about the Society or its members with anyone outside of the Society or other approved parties."

"I read that. But I don't sign contracts before my attorney reviews them."

I squeezed my eyes shut.

When I opened them, Cornelius was giving me a hard look. "We won't chop his head off, but we will certainly excise relevant memories."

That did *not* sound safe. Bradley was already weird enough; he didn't need anyone scrambling his brains with their voodoo memory excision tactics.

"Hey, Bradley, it's not really a contract. It's just a promise. Right?"

"That's what a contract is, Mallory." He sounded disappointed that I didn't already know that.

"Here's the thing: the alternatives to you not signing are pretty crappy. And it would be really upsetting for me if you didn't sign the confidentiality agreement, because then we can't work together."

I was pretty certain that elicited another growl from

Cornelius—but I was too worried about Bradley's scrambled brains to be too worried.

"I do want to be your sidekick," he said. I held my breath. "Okay. I'll sign it if I get to stay on your team."

I had a team? First I was a crime-fighting ninja vampire. And now I had a crime-fighting ninja team. Bradley really needed to get out more. "Sure thing."

Anton came back on the line, said, "He signed," and hung up.

"I think Anton hung up on me." I handed the phone back to Cornelius. "But he said Bradley signed."

"Good enough—for now. But if your friend becomes a problem, we'll be contacting you. You and your friends are a bother, Ms. Andrews."

And he didn't know about the dead body in Gladys's herb garden. Although Gladys really was more of a client. Mrs. A was a friend, but she could hardly help being a murder victim. Leave it to Cornelius to blame me for *that*. Alex—well, Alex had his own history with Cornelius that predated me. By a lot, I suspected. And we weren't exactly friends. Friendly, but not friends. Sort of friends. Whatever.

Okay—maybe my friends and I were a bother, if you looked at events in a very specific, very Cornelius sort of way.

Reading from his computer screen, Cornelius said, "Anton made a note that the app was created over six weeks ago. A good sign, since we would have seen the signs by now if it was public. We'll look for the usual: the app tying into sensational headlines, whisperings of conspiracies and cover-ups—that sort of thing. So long as it stays quiet for the next few months, we can assume we dodged a major reveal event." Cornelius turned his attention to me, and his eyes were liquid mercury again. "But if there's a whiff of this in the media, we'll be talking with you and your friend Bradley again."

And that was it. He booted us out of his office after that.

In the hallway, I turned to Alex and said, "Catastrophe averted?"

"Sure—six weeks ago. It's good news that it's been out of Bradley's hands for that length and nothing has surfaced. Very good news. Now Anton will work on finding the anonymous client—and shutting him up. And tracking down the exact dissemination venues and recipients of the app." He picked up the pace. "Come on. We have a meeting with Becky."

All that drama, and we didn't even get to see how it resolved. It would be up to Anton to chase down the secretive gamer and silence him. I wasn't sure how I felt about that. The "silencing" part sounded ominous.

"Ugh. After that—the whole silver eyes thing—I need a break." I perked up. "Or a coffee."

"Are you sure caffeine is a good idea?" Alex gave me a smirky, you-can't-hold-your-caffeine look. "Oh, and the eyes were all for you. He has complete control. Cornelius's eyes only bleed when he wants them to—a fact I know well."

"That manipulative turkey." I pointed down the hall to Alex's office.

He frowned but followed me. "Yes and no. It could still blow up. If that app goes wide, it's a problem. And even if it doesn't, all it takes is one person to realize the value of the information, and we have a crisis. At which point, the enhanced community will want blood. And you really should be worried for your friend if that happens."

"Do you people even understand the concept of justice? You make it sound as if Bradley did something wrong—which he didn't; he built an app using his client's notes. And you want to crucify him for basically not knowing that a secret society exists and then failing to protect the society he didn't know about." I marched down the hall, caught up in my righteous rant.

It took me a second to realize Alex was a few steps behind, texting on his phone, oblivious to my rant. Ranting really wasn't as satisfying when no one was listening.

He caught up. "Sorry. Was texting Becky to let her know we're running a few minutes behind. What did I miss?"

"Nothing." Because I had a sneaking suspicion Alex didn't miss much and he just didn't feel like dealing with my feelings about Bradley and his involvement with the Society's twisted version of policing.

"I should also have something that passes as food for you in my office." He moved out of kicking range and said, "You must be hungry."

Not-so-subtle code for I was cranky as an overtired toddler.

"You can't diminish my concerns."

"I'm not diminishing your concerns. I'm pointing out that those same concerns existed yesterday and the day before. Change in the Society is slow—like I've said before. And working yourself up about it when you're starving isn't constructive."

"It's not supposed to be constructive. It's a rant. I'm venting. I'm expressing my frustration and allowing my emotions an outlet."

Alex opened the door to his office for me. "Veggie juice?"

"Lord, yes." I was starving. I needed a stash of food in my car and in my purse. Basically anywhere I spent more than a passing moment. "But you're not diverting me from caffeine."

"Can I suggest you limit your consumption to one cup?"

"You can suggest all you like."

Caffeine made most vamps higher than a kite. I had the fortune to be partially immune. I had to consume *a lot* of caffeine to produce intoxicating effects. I knew from my hallucinatory experience after three French press pots that limiting my consumption to a reasonable amount wasn't a terrible idea. The effects could also be exacerbated by hunger, exhaustion, and probably some other factors I hadn't discovered yet.

But one cup would give me a little buzz—the regular kind that humans got—without making me see sounds or have visions of my dead Great-Auntie Lula. Maybe one cup was enough.

"About this Becky lady." I helped myself to a mug and started prepping my instant coffee. Beggars couldn't be choosey. "What do we think about her?"

"No clue what you think—except that she's bland. *I* think she's a hard worker, maybe a little in love with Dyson." His second comment was offhand, an afterthought.

"Not all women are secretly in love with their bosses. The idea is pretty insulting, actually." I stirred my coffee and then turned to find Alex holding a large container of veggie juice. My eyes bugged out. "Been shopping at the wholesale club?"

But I ditched my coffee and popped the top off that jug of awesome. A split second before I drank out of the mega-jug, I paused.

Alex handed me a glass with raised eyebrows. "And it's not insulting. She could do better. Than Dyson and the position. She's really sharp. So either she's not ambitious, or..."

"A little in a love with her boss." I wrinkled my nose. "Is it racist that I think the concept of a person made from another person's dead bits is gross?"

"Not racist, but bigoted. And women usually adore golems." At my disbelieving look, he clarified: "Golems are typically very attractive, both the men and the women."

I chugged my juice as I contemplated Alex's comment. I finished off the glass and asked, "So Dyson was attractive?"

"Objectively, I suppose so."

I refilled my glass and considered how that might play into his death. A jealous lover? Maybe even Becky? "Any ideas if he was faithful to his wife?"

"I don't know—but I doubt it." He walked over to the fridge and pulled out a banana. "Golems are usually players, but individuals vary and people make their own choices. We'll get a feel for his relationship with his wife tomorrow. I have an appointment with her in the morning."

I noticed he'd excluded me. A slip of the tongue or was I not supposed to go? Guess I'd find out.

"Are you almost ready?" Alex asked.

My coffee was probably cool enough to chug. I eyed it—no steam rising—took a sip, and couldn't help a moan. Coffee had been something I drank out of habit as a human. But as a vamp...heavenly. Even instant coffee qualified. I sighed—no time to savor it today.

I finished off the mug in record time. "Ready. Where are we meeting?"

"The orientation room."

"And remind me what exactly Becky is again." I headed over to the tiny kitchenette cubicle in the corner of the office and rinsed my mug and glass.

"Coyote."

"Oh—that's right. You never said what a coyote is."

Alex stood by the door, waiting. "I tried. You were going on about werecoyotes—wherever you got that idea—and then got sidetracked by the witch hat."

He opened the door for me as I approached.

"Right." It had been a gorgeous hat. "But what about coyotes?"

"Illusion, mild persuasion—they're great con artists and magicians."

"Great, so we're headed into a meeting with a con artist."

"No. We're headed into a meeting with a woman who has the skills of a decent con artist." Alex looked at me. "Huge difference."

"Right. And I do like magicians." We were approaching the back room where the orientation had been held. I paused. "Do we have a strategy?"

Alex leaned his head close. "We do." And then he kept walking.

Before I could ask what that strategy was exactly, he was opening the door to the orientation room. Nuts.

8

PRETTY COYOTES AND GUILTY CLIENTS

"Becky Taylor." She extended her hand without hesitation. That was new.

I found myself hesitant to shake her hand—maybe I was finally assimilating. I shook off the thought and grasped her fingers. "Mallory Andrews. I was in your orientation this morning."

She was a girly hand shaker, more fingers and less palm-to-palm contact, but she still had a quick, firm grasp. I tried not to let the finger shake set my first impression of her.

"That's right. You had a call...an emergency, perhaps?" The inquiry was polite, but her eyes held a sharpness that was definitely criticism.

Honey-blonde hair in a sleek updo, a feminine, well-tailored suit that cost more than the contents of my recently acquired and much more casual wardrobe, and a professionally bland yet mildly interested look... How had I not noticed any of this when she'd been presenting the orientation materials this morning?

I narrowed my eyes. I wasn't technically a trained observer, but I was a formerly successful professional woman in a male-dominated industry. I was no slouch in the observation department. Which meant...someone used their sneaky illusion and persuasion skills maybe a little more routinely than she should.

"Not exactly." I leaned closer in a confidential way, curious to see how she'd respond. I lowered my voice as if sharing a secret. "A needy client. You know how those are."

And I'd swear I saw a flare of...some emotion before her polite mask was once more firmly fixed. "Orientation is a very important part of becoming a Society member. You need to make sure that you attend the rescheduled meeting."

"Absolutely. Will I get an email?"

Alex cleared his throat. "About Dyson..."

Becky turned to Alex with a downright feline smile. What was it with him and women? "Of course. You'll want his schedule. I'm sure he's just taking a break. Getting away from the pressures of governance. He works so hard." As she spoke, she pulled out her phone and tapped away. Flashing a sexy kitten smile at Alex, she said, "There. I've sent you a copy of his schedule for the last week. Will that do?"

"Very helpful, thank you," Alex said. But he didn't return her flirty smile or encourage her.

I made a mental note to quiz him on the way out. He wasn't usually shy with women, even when we were working. In fact, he'd been pretty insistent when we'd last worked together that he not miss his hot date. Actually, dates. There'd been a few with the same woman, if I remembered correctly. What happened to her? Maybe they were an item now? That would explain his disinterest in Becky—but then again, he had teased about handing his number out at the Divorced Divas party.

"Do you have any thoughts on where Dyson would go, if he did decide to take an unplanned vacation?" Alex asked.

"The coast, maybe? There are a few spa resorts he's particularly fond of—but he's never scheduled them without letting anyone know." Becky flipped through her contacts and tapped the screen, and Alex's phone pinged.

"Do you know why he wouldn't have told you, his wife, or his daughter that he was taking a vacation?" I asked sweetly. Because please—the man was dead. And how in the world would the woman who runs his life, as Ms. Becky Taylor clearly did, not know that—or at least suspect it?

"I'm not sure about his daughter, but his wife? I wouldn't be surprised if she knew nothing. They aren't particularly close right now." She turned to Alex. "You know how it is—long marriages ebb and flow. Theirs is currently ebbing."

"How long have they been married?" Alex asked.

Becky shrugged. "Two, two and a half? Maybe longer. They were already married when I joined Mr. Dyson."

I squinted. Not years. Surely she meant decades, because the alternative—centuries—was too difficult to wrap my head around.

"But it's not typical for him to leave without informing you of his plans," Alex said.

"Not for any length of time, and certainly not if he planned to miss a meeting. But I can't imagine... Well, he's hardly been kidnapped, has he? We haven't seen a ransom demand. And—the other—it's simply too terrible to contemplate." Her lower jaw quivered with emotion and her eyes had the sheen of imminent tears.

Alex gave her a second to compose herself.

"I'm sorry," she said. "I've convinced myself he's simply off on holiday for a bit. I'm sure that's all this is. Anything else... It's simply not thinkable."

"I understand. I know you've worked with him a long time. If you think of anything, please let us know." Alex lifted his phone. "And if I have questions about his schedule, I'll be in touch. Thank you for your time."

"He is going to be fine, isn't he? He's a golem, and they're awfully difficult to..." She took a breath, and with it recaptured her composure. Her face, once again, held that politely interested look. "Anything I can do, just let me know."

Alex nodded and then opened the door for me. When we were out in the hall, he held a finger to his lips.

The silence was killing me. By the time we were back in the hallway with Alex's office, he was trotting to keep up with me, and he had a good six inches or more on me.

I opened his office door and turned around. "Well? Why are you not into the flirtatious Becky?"

"That's your first question. Are you kidding me?"

"What? That's bizarre behavior for you. So spill—what's up?"

"I have a particular dislike of persuasion. I'm sure I don't have to explain to you why."

If I had spirits whispering vile suggestions in my ear every time I was a little tired or getting a cold, I'd be pretty done with magical persuasion, too. "Gotcha—but how did you know?"

Alex ran a hand through his hair. "It's difficult to spot, but with practice it can be done."

What he didn't have to say was that he had a lot of practice. I felt a tug in the general region of my heart—pretty sure it was my heart. Could have been my stomach. As I retrieved some veggie juice from his fridge, I started to recap the short interview. If her flirty, sexy smile had some magical push behind it... "What about her teary-eyed display? Was that some kind of show as well?"

"No. the tears were genuine. But, then again, the flirtatious smile was a hundred percent real. Persuasion impacts how the recipient perceives a certain image, idea, or suggestion. *Illusion* changes that image, idea, or suggestion to something other than what it is."

"Huh. So the tears were real, and she wasn't using her magic to enhance them in any way?"

Alex raised his eyebrows. "No. She was actually sad, and the tears were real. Is that so hard to imagine? The woman has worked with Dyson for decades."

"Yeah, I guess. She just flipped from one to the other so fast...and I kinda want to not like her. Is that weird?"

"I'm with you on that. I don't appreciate it when anyone uses persuasion on me—small pushes or not." His face took on a hard cast as he spoke.

My phone rang, breaking the tension—because there was some crackling in the air. I made a mental note never to use persuasion on Alex should the occasion ever arise. Which it wouldn't...because I didn't have that particular bit of magic.

"Hello?"

I'd answered without checking the caller, so I was a little surprised to hear Bradley's voice. "I've sent you an email."

"Uh, thanks, Bradley. I'll have a look in a bit."

"About your case."

"Ooooh! Of course. Sorry—and thank you. Did you find something good?"

"It's in the email. Bye." And he hung up.

I looked at my phone and shook my head.

After a few taps, I saw why he'd called. The email gave

very specific instructions that I should reply when I received it. As soon as I received it. Or he'd call.

I chuckled as I opened the attachment. That was Bradley. And then I saw the contents. "Ohmygod. We have to meet with Mrs. Dyson."

"We will. We have an appointment tomorrow. Didn't I already tell you that?" Alex had migrated to his futon and was kicking back, feet on the coffee table, eating an apple.

I plopped down on the futon next to Alex and showed him the spreadsheet Bradley had put together.

Alex took my phone, blew up the image, and scrolled.

"He could have just sent a summary, saying Mrs. Ophelia Dyson was up to her eyeballs in credit card debt—but he probably thought we'd want to see the numbers." I hopped up and retrieved my abandoned glass of veggie juice.

"How did he get this information so quickly?" Alex asked.

I wiped my mouth and shrugged. "Maybe better not to ask? But it's helpful, right?"

"It's helpful so long as he didn't leave some traceable trail. I can certainly get this type of information...but it takes time and effort, so he might have saved us—me—some legwork."

I sat back down next to him, careful not to spill my juice. "Well, either way, this totally gives her a motive. If Mr. Dyson has all the cash, and Mrs. Dyson spends more than she has, then she would want him dead so she could inherit the estate."

"What makes you think he has all the money?"

"Well, she doesn't, and if he doesn't... Oh, now there's a thought. Maybe they're broke? Because that's a motive all its own. Maybe Dyson was super pissed that she spent them into poverty, and then they got into a massive fight, and she killed him." I nodded. I could totally see that happening.

"Right. Based on what facts? And what about this murder says crime of passion? We're looking for someone who had time to plan. That's just wild speculation."

I wasn't convinced I was wildly speculating. Massive debt and disagreements over money had pushed couples to violence innumerable times. Why not this time? Although... "I suppose the murderer did actually want the body found. There were certainly better ways to completely dispose of it. Assuming golem corpses can be destroyed just like any other corpses?"

Alex nodded and took another bite of his apple.

"Still, I do think you can have a passionate motive for a planned murder."

"Maybe." Alex didn't sound like he bought into that theory. "Regardless of who did it, why dump the body at Gladys's house? A frame-up is the only reasonable conclusion."

"Ha! And Ophelia would need to frame someone because the wife is always a suspect." I considered the ever-loyal Becky. "Yeah, I'm not sure the frame-up theory applies equally as well to Becky." I brightened when I considered the other possibilities. "But it would be relevant if we discover Dyson had any business or political enemies."

"You're having a little too much fun with this case." Alex elbowed me. "Keep a lid on the wild speculation—at least until we have a chance to speak with Ophelia and Rachael tomorrow—and try to keep a somewhat open mind."

I realized all of a sudden that my left side was toasty warm and my right was hyper-cooled by the air conditioning. I looked at Alex. "Do you run, like, ten degrees warmer than humans?" A nasty thought occurred. "Oh no, nononono. Am I all chilly and clammy now that I'm a vamp?"

Why had that never occurred to me? I wasn't *exactly* dead. But I also wasn't precisely alive. I mean, I didn't age. Living things aged.

"Stop." Alex snapped his fingers in front of my face.

I set my juice down. "Don't snap your fingers at me."

"Then don't act like a hysterical nitwit." He held out his hand. "Give me your hand."

Reluctantly, and with a suspicious look, I gave him my hand.

He wrapped his hand around mine. "I'm probably two to three degrees warmer than you, because your circulation has slowed down—" He squeezed my hand tight when I went to yank it away. "Not much different than any other woman with low blood pressure. But I'm also a little warmer." He let my hand go suddenly. "Something to do with the ties I have to the spirit world. Probably because it puts my magic on a constant slow burn. Most people don't notice it."

"Ah. I guess you do eat a lot."

He grunted. "*I* eat a lot?"

I flicked his shoulder. "You're not supposed to mention how much a lady eats."

He took a breath to respond but was cut off by my phone ringing. He handed my phone back and said, "Wembley."

Why did I have a niggling feeling I'd done something wrong?

I tapped the screen. "What's up, Wembley?"

"The appointment you missed with the decorator—that's what. The kitchen? You're supposed to be picking out tile and gorgeous new appliances." He sounded more than a little peeved.

"Oh, I am so sorry. I totally forgot." I perked up when I remembered my new resolution. "But I have a plan for that. I'm going to start scheduling everything on my calendar app."

There was a deafening silence.

"Wembley?"

"I'm trying to understand how someone raised in the modern age could be so removed from any form of schedule. And how a formerly overbooked professional could not understand how to use calendar reminders."

"Ah." There wasn't an excuse, I realized with a twinge of guilt. "It's the new me. Or it was. Now there's a *new* new me. I'm embracing my calendar. And calendar reminders. I promise to be much better in future."

"Excellent. Then you can make the next meeting I've arranged. The poor woman has agreed to return in an hour, so get your butt home now. This kitchen won't pick out its own countertops."

I smiled, thinking about my nifty new kitchen. "I'm on it." After I ended the call, I stood up and said to Alex, "Minor detour. I have to stop at the house for an appointment."

"Good. Try to get some rest while you're at it. We have a long night ahead." He stretched out on the futon. "Shut the lights off on the way out."

"Yeah, but before I go..." All of that talk about his magic had reminded me of something I'd meant to ask. There didn't seem to be a good time, so the present would have to do. "Speaking of your...you know...your—"

"The spirit entities that like to harass me?"

"Yeah, them. Did you ask them about Dyson? I mean, if there were any hanging around Gladys's place—which I'm sure there weren't. But if there were, did you ask if they saw who killed him?"

"They said Gladys did it—but they seemed confused and weren't sure."

"What?" I lowered my voice back down from a screech. "What does that mean?"

"I have no clue—which is why I didn't share it. They don't usually lie, but they can be ambiguous, vague, uncooperative, and all other sorts of a pain in my backside."

I glared, but he ignored me.

"Lights."

I flicked off the lights, but also pulled the door shut with more force than necessary. How could he think I wouldn't want information about Gladys? Especially possibly incriminating evidence?

As I drove home in my wonderful new-to-me Jeep Grand Cherokee, I figured it must not be that incriminating—or he would have said. Surely he would have said?

9

TANGWYSTL, COME!

I'd stewed all the way home about the whole Gladys-could-be-the-murderer omission. Alex could be infuriating sometimes. Just because he'd ruled out the information was no reason not to share it with me. We could talk about it. Maybe decide together that it was useless rubbish. Or that our client was an evil mastermind and completely brilliant at deception.

At least Wembley was upfront and honest with me.

I unlocked the front door with my key. Oh, right, *he hadn't been*. Einarr. Who was this Einarr guy? Army of one, undead warrior—either way, it was enough to blow my mind.

And yet I'd forgotten about it until I walked in the house. Because my Wembley was squishy around the middle and didn't like swords. He used a gun because swords were difficult and a lot of work—his words. How *that guy* was an undead warrior of Norse legend...

"Wembley!"

He meandered into the front hall, and I took stock. His hippie beard was looking much more groomed these days.

Ever since he'd taken my mom to that fundraising luncheon, it had been tidier. He'd been tidier. The flip-flops were now one of a few pairs of shoes he wore—before they'd been his single choice for footwear. He still wore the dark green cargo shorts—a lot—but I'd seen him in long pants at least once.

Actually, now that I thought about it, maybe I should be worried. My mother could not date a vampire. And certainly not a vampire named Einarr.

"Why are you yelling at me? I should be the one hollering; you missed an appointment with your decorator. Do you want me to live here forever?"

That put a stop to the snit I was about to throw. Because I kinda did.

"First you yell," he said, "and now you stand there staring like a zombie. Make up your mind."

I weighed which of the various problems were topmost in my mind...then reshuffled and figured out which was the lowest-hanging fruit. "I hear you're coming with us tonight to dig—"

"Tscht." He lifted a hand. "My Spanish-speaking contractors only pretend they don't speak great English."

"Ah. You coming?"

"For sure. Wouldn't miss it." He turned around and headed toward the kitchen. "Hungry?"

"Yes!" I started to jog in the direction of the kitchen.

"I found some vegan cheese you might like to try." I slowed to a crawl, but Wembley's excitement didn't waver. "I'm thinking we melt it, and you can try a spoonful. Sort of a liquid, right? It took a few tries, but I found one that melts well."

He really was trying to broaden my culinary horizons. And also to find something that actually filled me up. We'd had a few conversations about his diet, and I was shocked to learn how little blood he needed to survive. And even more depressing, it didn't take much more than that to really fill him up. There was a reason the guy had acquired a little belly over the years. I guessed all that sword-fighting had kept him trim before.

"Alex said you'd be upset, but we're friends—right?" He nodded, looking more amused than concerned, so I asked, "And you wouldn't want me wandering around thinking things that weren't right? Or having unanswered questions?"

He rolled his eyes at the last part. "Go on. What do you want to know?"

"Einarr?" I closed one eye and waited.

And he laughed. "Alex said that would upset me? It's an old name. A really old name."

"So you used to be him? Army of one or undead warrior guy."

Wembley scratched his beard. "More like a warrior who fought like he had nothing to live for. Unafraid of death. That name goes all the way back to my pre-vamp days." He whispered "pre-vamp" as he pulled a suspiciously aromatic package out of the fridge. Wiggling it like a treat for a dog, he said, "Vegan cheese. You know you're excited."

I tried not to wrinkle my nose—but there was only so much a girl could do when even her nose hairs were retreating from the stench. "Why would he think it would bother you to talk about it?"

"It might have at some point. But it was all so long ago—it doesn't matter anymore." Wembley chopped a small wedge of the cheese into tiny pieces. "And the past clings with more determination to Alex than it does to me." He shrugged, placing a ceramic bowl with the cheese bits into the microwave. "Possibly because he's younger."

"Any chance you were a Viking?"

Wembley grinned. "Now where would you get that idea?"

"Google." I propped a hip against the counter. This was going to take a while. "Come on, give me a hint. I mean, the name is Norse, and I know you're a super-old dude."

"Now you're just trying to be mean. I've got news for you: being old in the land of vamps isn't an insult."

I actually did know that age was power in the vamp world. I also knew that, unlike in the mundane world, the advantage applied equally to men and women. Bonus for me. "So...about Einarr?"

"Like I said, my name before I ever was bitten. There's not much story to tell. I was basically a drugged-out soldier until I was turned. Once I was a vamp, I didn't need the high to fight. I was the Viking equivalent of a super soldier, a Berserker. Maybe you've heard the term?" The microwave timer dinged, but Wembley didn't move.

I was still trying to digest the part about drugs when he pulled out the big guns. "Sorry, Berserker? As in killed anyone within weapon rage, impervious to injury, mad fighting skills, unbelievable strength—"

"Yeah, yeah. It was the drugs." He shrugged. "Except for the mad fighting skills. Those we acquired through hours and hours of training. The rest...drugs."

"You fought while you were high?"

"Yep."

That required some mental shifting and rearranging. I didn't typically envision Vikings as a bunch of tokers. "That was normal back then?"

"Not at all. But among a certain elite soldier—it was the norm."

"Right." I crossed my arms and considered how this

affected my perception of Viking history. I'd have to think on it a bit. "What exactly were you high on?"

"I'm not sure. Some concoction they gave us. A hallucinogenic stimulant. Perception was altered, distancing you from the things you were doing, and, let me tell you, I was feeling no pain."

"You sound kind of okay with all of that?"

"No, not really. But like I said, it was a long time ago. And eventually, after I became a vamp, I stopped fighting."

"Oh, that's the thing you were saying about not training anymore."

"No, that was after Vietnam."

I took a deep breath, which was a bad idea because I got a snoot full of stinky cheese. "You gave up fighting, but only after you fought in Vietnam."

Wembley sighed. "I've given up the sword—literally and metaphorically—several times over the years. It's a hard habit to kick, especially when you're a member of a violent society."

I snorted. "That's the truth. The Society's wonky justice system alone makes me cringe. Then you add in—"

"No, you misunderstand. I mean human society. But you're not wrong about the Society's justice system. I only wish I could believe that Lemann is as committed to change as he says."

Cornelius Lemann, the Society for the Study of Occult and Paranormal Phenomenon's chief operating officer, a.k.a. Wembley's nemesis. In Wembley's mind.

"Cornelius isn't so bad."

"I hope you're right." Wembley pulled the now even more aromatic cheese from the microwave.

"So you've been a hippie since Vietnam, embracing

peace, love, light..." But then again, Wembley still had a gun and wasn't hesitant to use it.

"Hardly. I haven't been a *soldier* since Nam. As a vamp, self-defense is always important. Your progenitor getting the drop on me was a serious kick in the pants."

"Well, he was a mind-reading, super-fast vamp." My lips twisted in sympathy over the indignity of being knocked unconscious by a much younger—though freakishly fast—vamp.

"Alex was thrilled to have a proficient, if rusty, training partner again."

"Hm." I was tempted to ask exactly how old Alex was—but I restrained myself. He wouldn't appreciate me prying. "I'm glad you're back in the game, Wembley. That bit about the drugs is depressing, though. Although I guess societies throughout the ages have exploited what advantages they could during times of conflict."

Wembley shrugged then retrieved the bowl from the microwave. "Cheese?"

I frowned at the little ceramic bowl and the melted goo it held. "How is this helpful again?"

Wembley settled himself in a chair adjacent to mine. "If you can tolerate this, I'm going to try for some vegan cheese soup. I thought it might make a nice change for you, especially as it gets colder. You know, in December or January."

I chuckled. "Love that two-month Texas winter, don't you?" But my heart also danced in my chest for the second time that day. Wembley was trying—really putting some effort in—to make me more comfortable in my vamp skin. I steeled myself and tried the goo.

"I think I can work with the flavor—if you can just keep it down." Wembley looked at me anxiously.

"Good. I think." I counted to five. Usually five seconds was more than enough. "Yeah. I can do this."

"All right, then. I'll start experimenting with a vegan cheese soup." Wembley's blue eyes hardened. "So how did you stumble on Einarr? I think there's a story you're avoiding."

I considered if this was a NSFC—not safe for contractors—conversation, then figured I could wing it. "Bradley was commissioned by a gamer to create an app to accompany a new game he was developing. All super hush-hush."

"Bradley that you have tea with every week?"

I nodded. "You saw him at Mrs. A's funeral. The really uptight guy that didn't speak to anyone?"

"Right, I remember him. With the bow tie."

"Yep, that was him. Einarr is one of the characters in the app. There's a picture." I glanced at Wembley's midsection.

"Humph." His formerly bushy and now neatly trimmed eyebrows beetled together. "Training like that eats up your whole day. And if there aren't heads to be chopped and threats around every corner... But like I already said, I'm back to training." He patted his recently slimmer midsection.

"But I'm guessing no all-day-long training sessions. Not that I'm dissing your training schedule. Since I only spend about four or five hours a week practicing with Tangwystl, I can hardly say anything."

"And you're attempting to master a new skill." He grunted his disapproval. "You should practice more."

"Seriously? But you're missing the point. The app? You do know what an app is, don't you?"

Wembley snagged my half-eaten and now cooled cheese. "You're the one who can't set a simple calendar reminder. I am completely up to date on apps. The long and short is that Alex—and Cornelius, who I'm sure is involved in this up to his mercury eyeballs—are both young. They haven't lived through as many reveal scares as I have." He returned to the table and sat back down. Very quietly, he said, "Humans don't *want* to know, and that is to our great advantage."

I wasn't sure if that thought comforted vamp me or disturbed my remaining human sensibilities—but either way, I thought Wembley was likely right. Pockets of information might be released, and while those pockets might be more dangerous in the digital age, if humans didn't want to know...that made the secret easier to keep.

"Tell me about the Dyson family."

Wembley wiggled his eyebrows. "Well, I'm not much for gossip, but I hear..."

And Wembley heard a lot. The marriage wasn't just going through a slump; it was dying a painfully slow death. One so slow, it spanned several decades. Rachael was a good kid and practical, but tired of dealing with her parents' silliness. She still lived at home, but word on the street was that she planned to move out soon. Soon being relative—that could mean six months or six years, I discovered. And Ophelia's shopping habits were no secret.

All in all, not bad information gathering for a kitchen-table chat. Wembley ran out of scoop about two minutes before the decorator had come back. Then I had a very productive session with her, as well. We decided on a retro look for the bathroom and picked out tile and fixtures. And for the kitchen, we decided on slate counter tops, mostly green with some purple. A little off the beaten path, but it felt fun and right for the space. A pretty productive afternoon, all in all.

Ten minutes after the decorator left, I rolled over in my

borrowed bed. If I could get all of Wembley's knowledge to settle in my brain long enough to fall asleep and catch a quick nap, that would be great. Because I had both the Dysons' lives and my nifty new kitchen-to-be swirling around in my brain, and I needed to catch a quick nap before our garden raid.

Or whatever digging up a dead guy in the middle of the night should be called.

What seemed like seconds after I laid my head down on my pillow, I heard someone say, "Wake up."

No way. I just went to bed. I pulled my pillow over my head.

"Eeep." A nasty pinch on my upper arm had me chucking that same pillow at my attacker.

"Get your butt out of that bed now, or I'm leaving you here." Alex held the pillow I'd thrown under his left arm.

"Nuts. What are you doing here so early?" Then I looked out of the newly repaired window—the one my progenitor had smashed through not so long ago. It was pitch black outside.

Sweeping my hand around in the sheets for my phone, I tried to remember if I'd set my alarm.

Alex cleared his throat. In his right hand, he held my phone. "The alarm was going when I walked in. After knocking." He must have seen my disbelieving frown, because he added, "Loudly."

"Hmph. Sorry. Get lost. I'll be ready in five."

As he walked out the door, Alex said, "There's coffee in the kitchen."

I was ready in three, and that even included brushing my teeth. Even though vamps don't have plaque or, apparently, bad breath, I clung to the very human habit. Because not brushing my teeth...just ew.

"Coffee?" I said as I walked into the kitchen in my black jeans, T-shirt, and All Stars.

Alex looked me up and then down. "Your shoes have a lot of white on them."

I looked at the splashes of white on my black sneakers. "Oh..."

Wembley handed me a cup of coffee. "He's kidding."

"Hey, not cool. I woke up four minutes ago. I'm not equipped." But then I had a sip of hot vampire crack and everything was all right again. I sighed.

"Come on." Alex jingled his keys. "Star won't wait up all night for us."

Now that I had my coffee, I was in a much more expansive mood. So much so, that I figured asking who Star was could wait until we were in the car. I tipped my travel mug at Wembley in thanks and said, "Yes, sir. Let's boogie."

Alex sighed. "Tangwystl?"

"Right." I'd forgotten that I was going to start carrying her around. To get used to the feel of carrying a sword, but also because we were going to dig up a dead body. Perhaps a little sketchy and certainly containing an element of danger. I imagined having the reassuring weight of her in my hand would make me feel more comfortable.

Wembley was already heading to my bedroom to retrieve her by the time I'd processed what Alex had said.

But then she appeared. In my hand.

I almost dropped my coffee. Almost.

"What the devil?" Alex looked at the sword and then at me.

With coffee in my right hand and sword in my left, I stood there, probably looking like a gaping idiot. Because I didn't have a clue what had just happened.

10

WHICH WHAT?

"Uh..." I made a sweeping motion with Tangwystl. Yep. It was her, and she was really in my hand. "Hm."

"Care to explain?" Alex asked.

Apparently the look of bafflement that I thought was on my face wasn't.

Wembley returned with my scabbard in his hand. "Where's your sword? Oh." He cocked his head. "How'd that happen?"

"Um, we should hurry? Star won't wait up all night for us?" I gave the guys a weak smile then snatched the scabbard out of Wembley's hand and sheathed Tangwystl.

Alex opened the front door. "We'll talk in the car—because we *are* talking about this."

Nuts. That meant my magical sword landing in my hand—literally appearing from the ether—was exactly as weird as I thought.

"Hm." I figured noncommittal was good, since I could hardly commit to giving info I didn't have. I slung her across my back and headed out the door. Maybe they could explain it to me. I brightened. Their collective age and knowledge was, after all, much, much greater than my own.

"Wembley, any thoughts?" I asked after I'd climbed into Alex's Juke.

"Don't look at me," Wembley said. "I didn't have a clue she could do that."

Alex climbed in the driver's seat and then said, "Ask the sword. Her English is passable, isn't it?"

I decided there was no reason to comment on my sword's less-than-stellar communication skills.

"So, Tangwystl, what do you have to say for yourself?" When I'd settled into the back seat, I laid her across my lap and ran my fingers over the hilt.

Not it

"It's not a game. I just need to know how you did it. I mean, that's pretty handy. I'd like to be able to do it again, especially in a pinch."

You. Not me. Not it.

Ugh.

Wembley looked over his shoulder. "What does she have to say for herself?"

"Not much other than it wasn't her. Which is clearly wrong, because how else does that happen?"

Deafening silence followed my question.

"Guys?"

Wembley cleared his throat. "You wanna say it, or should I?"

"Neither of us says it. Neither of us thinks it." Alex sounded grim. "So, we're meeting Star in about two hours, which means we're already behind. I figure we'll get to Gladys's house about a quarter after midnight. We'll need to push to get the body out fast. Star is not a night person."

I was tempted to take the bait. I would like to know who

this Star woman was. And then, naturally, come back to the weird sword thing. No way I was leaving that question unanswered. But a creepy feeling was pushing in on me. I needed to know what they were avoiding—preferably now.

"First you want to talk about my sword's exhibitionist stunt; now you don't. Clearly you buy her story and don't think it's a part of her normal magic routine. And suddenly that's off limits. You're freaking me out."

As I waited for an answer, I rubbed my thumb across Tangwystl's hilt. It was comforting.

But neither of the guys was talking, and we were almost to Gladys's house. "Hey? What are you both so afraid to say?"

Which

"Which what?" I asked my sword. If I knew how to teach a sword a broader vocabulary, I would. But apparently her former partners hadn't spoken English and she was just kind of picking it up on her own.

The tension crackled in the car.

"What?" I leaned forward between the front seats. "What?"

Alex glanced at me and snapped, "Put your seatbelt on."

"Witch," Wembley said. "W-I-T-C-H."

"I still don't get it."

Alex pulled into Gladys's driveway. "Not now. And not in front of Gladys. We'll talk about it later."

I sighed. "Is this one of those things I'm not supposed to mention to anyone?"

Alex tipped his head back against the headrest.

Wembley perked up. If he were a hound, his ears would have pricked. "What other things are you not supposed to mention?"

Oops.

I sighed quietly. "Apparently there's a growing list. I'll let you know if I ever decide to go public."

"A mystery wrapped in a...well, you know." Wembley opened the passenger door, climbed out, and shut it quietly.

Alex didn't turn around. "Witches learn their craft. The longer they study and practice, the more magic finds and attaches to them. It's a transformation, but of a different kind than a vampire's."

"Okay—but I haven't done any of that. I would know if I had, right?"

"Yeah—exactly. But the green-blue sparkles, the bitter tears, and now the ability to call your sword—it all reeks of witch magic." Alex finally turned to look at me. "And that isn't possible."

Would the weirdness of my transformation never end? I almost wished I was the normal, blood-drinking kind of vamp. But at the thought of blood—worse yet, ingesting blood—my stomach protested. Maybe the vegan gig with all its issues was cool.

He got out of the car, and, like Wembley, carefully and quietly closed the door. Sure, we were on a timetable, but I thought he was mostly running away from my questions.

"Tangwystl, I think we're in a little bit of trouble."

Cheerfully, she said: *Stab-stabby*.

"Yeah, not that kind."

She blew a raspberry.

Apparently all trouble was the stabby kind in Tangwystl's world.

Before I opened the car door, I had a thought. "I don't suppose I can use you to dig?"

She sighed as I opened the door.

No fun. Can do.

In a whisper, I said, "Well, we'll save that as a last resort."

It did seem a little shameful to use my magical sword that loved stabbing and slicing people to dig around in the soil—even if it was to dig up a dead body. When my eyes adjusted to the dark, I saw that Alex and Wembley both had folding shovels. Alex must have popped the hatch and pulled them out as I'd been chitchatting with my sword.

I whispered very close to her hilt—what I thought of as her epicenter or the brains of the operation. "I think you're safe."

Tss-hee-hee.

Which sounded a lot like a child's excited, burbling laugh.

I slung her over my back and followed the guys to the front door. Before anyone knocked, it swung open, revealing a dark interior and no person.

Was it just me, or was that super creepy at midnight thirty?

Then Gladys's bodiless voice emerged from the interior. "Come inside."

The three of us piled into her foyer looking guilty as all heck. Once the door shut behind us, she flipped on a lamp situated on the credenza near the door. The muted lamp revealed that Gladys was clothed similarly to me—in black from head to toe. She'd even wrapped a dark scarf around her mass of bright red hair.

Looking at her, I could see how the guys might have thought I was being a little ridiculous. It was a tiny bit over the top for the late night gardening we were supposedly doing.

Right, because there was nothing odd or suspicious about midnight gardening.

Gladys eyed my getup. "That's a nice look on you."

Actually, it was on her, as well. Black didn't wash out her

pale skin, just made her look dramatic and mysterious. "Right back at you."

Alex cleared his throat. "If you guys are done...?"

"Right, of course." Gladys ushered us through the house to the back door. We exited onto her patio, where she had fairy lights hung along the deck. "Ah, I didn't want to turn them off because they're always on after dark."

I looked deeper into the yard and could see that the lights did nothing to illuminate the herb garden.

Alex gave her a thumbs-up and we headed toward the herb garden, a.k.a. Dyson's not-final resting place.

Gladys had very carefully removed each of the plants and placed them back into their original pots. They were lined up in a row off to the side, waiting to be replanted, I was sure. I shuddered. I didn't get how she could dig around in that soil, knowing what was there, and not be completely freaked out.

Thankfully, I didn't have to do much digging. After watching Wembley and Alex hard at it for five minutes, it was clear that digging up a body was really hard work. And I wasn't the vampiest vampire. In fact, I was pretty puny by vamp standards. Drinking blood had some distinct advantages, including increased strength and stamina; no blood meant I missed out on those particular enhancements.

Gladys, on the other hand, was all about consuming blood and had received the corresponding strength and stamina. But she was busy keeping the mess to a minimum and wasn't digging. I eyed her efforts: not bad. With any luck, the end result of this little adventure wouldn't resemble a grave-robbing expedition. With some luck and Gladys's diligent attention, it would look like a normal herb garden when we finished.

Only two people could dig at a time, so puny me was left

to supervise and act as relief digger.

Just my luck that Alex had stopped for a drink when we hit Dyson. When *I* hit Dyson. With a squishy thud. Okay, he didn't really squish. But in my mind's eye, I could see his body rotting apart into its constituent bits. I tried not to hurl, because eww. I really wished I'd never learned what a golem was.

Alex's hand on my shoulder brought me back to reality and from the brink of puking all over the grave. I stepped back from the pit and let him and Wembley do the nastiest part, removing the last handfuls of soil covering our cadaver.

As we pulled him up—that was a task made much easier with four people—I was reminded that Gladys had had the forethought to wrap him in an old sheet. So it wasn't nearly as disgusting or as difficult as it could have been. Still, a dead body was an unwieldy package, and we were all glad to have four sets of hands.

I stared at the tightly wrapped, body-shaped package now lying on the ground next to a huge hole in the ground. I tensed, as if at any moment the spotlights would shine, the police helicopter would do a flyover, and we'd be called out on our nefarious actions.

Silence followed. Very dark, very still silence. And I relaxed.

"Eep!" I squeaked.

A hand on my arm made me jump—thankfully away from the hole we'd dug and not into it. Heart thudding, I looked at the four-foot-deep hole. I didn't think my nerves could have handled that.

Alex made a shushing noise close to my ear. A shiver went up my spine, and I wasn't quite sure if it was fear, attraction, or some freaky combination of both. I shook his hand off my arm. Not his fault I was wigging—but better for all concerned if he wasn't touching me.

Then I realized he, Wembley, and Gladys were all waiting for me. It was time to pick up the package. I was liking that word more and more. Better not to think about what was in the package.

I steeled myself and then nodded.

As a coordinated effort, it was quite simple. And while I suspected any of the three of my co-conspirators could easily have slung him—ah, the package—over their shoulder, it would have made a heck of a soil-smudging mess.

Except for my squeak of dismay, we'd worked silently up to that point. So when I realized there was no way Dyson's corpse would fit in the Juke, I got a little panicky. Surely someone had thought of that? Much as the words wanted to spill out of my mouth, I kept my silence as we carried him around to the side of the house.

Then Gladys stepped away from Dyson's feet, leaving Wembley to bear that burden, and opened the side door to her garage. I almost melted in relief. Gladys had a Volvo Cross Country wagon. Thank goodness someone with some planning skills had made that call.

And thank goodness for whatever weird twist of fate had Gladys keeping the Volvo wagon and not the sporty little Mercedes in the divorce settlement. The wagon had been her husband's weekend vehicle. He'd kept both his commuter sedan and her Mercedes. I wasn't sure if Gladys held a secret love for the Volvo, or her husband had and she'd done it to screw him, or neither and he'd simply left her with the car he was least fond of. Either way—yay for the wagon and its dead body...uh, package-hauling capabilities.

We trooped inside the garage, managing to get through

the door without too much fuss. Once the door was closed behind us, Gladys turned on the garage light.

"Oh boy," I said, eyeing the mess we'd made in her garage with our soil-covered...package.

"It's fine. I have a cleanup plan." She popped the hatch on the wagon.

Since she'd backed it into the garage, we didn't have far to go at all.

"Just put him on that sheet there and then we can slide it further into the car." She tipped her head. "With him on it, of course."

I blinked. She was so calm. Why was that thought so disturbing? Then I remembered—Alex's spirits and their confused proclamation about Gladys. I'd forgotten amidst the sleeping and waking suddenly, and the witch thing, and then the dead body/package.

But no. Just—no. I had to have some reality in which to ground myself. And I chose the reality in which Gladys was not a cold-blooded killer. Because that was the way it had to be for now.

We followed the very innocent, definitely framed Gladys's instructions and got the package into the car. I really didn't know how murderers dealt with dead bodies. It was all so complicated. I stopped. "This is all really complicated."

"Alex stopped by around ten and we worked out the details. I came up with the transport and cleanup plans." Gladys looked really proud of herself. "I even blacked out the garage windows." She pointed to the tiny windows located in the garage door that were all black.

Because the neighbors wouldn't notice that. I shook my head. "No, that's not what I meant. Although good job with the planning. No, I mean, the murderer had to get Dyson's body here somehow. Did he or she have help? If they did it alone—how?"

Alex closed the hatch of the wagon and pulled out his phone. After a quick glance, he said, "All valid questions that I'd be glad to discuss with you en route. We're behind schedule, and—"

"I know, I know. Star isn't a night person." I shook my head. I was interested to meet this Star lady. "Who's driving what and where?"

Wembley lifted the Juke's keys. "I'm headed home."

Alex must have passed off his keys when I wasn't paying attention.

"You and I are headed to see Star," Alex said. "I figured you'd pitch a fit if I tried to send you home."

True. But I just smiled and tried not to think about exactly what we were going to do, because...ick.

"And I'm on cleanup duty." Gladys handed her keys over to Alex. "Someone will drop the car off tomorrow before noon?"

"I'll make sure of it. You won't miss yoga."

Gladys smiled at Alex. "Perfect. Off you go, then." She waited until both Alex and I were in the Volvo then shut off the lights.

Alex hit the garage door opener, Wembley headed for the Juke, and we followed him down the drive and out onto the street.

"It's like a choreographed dance. There are a lot of moving pieces to this."

Alex turned the headlights on after he'd gone a few houses past Gladys's. "Yeah. I'm with you. Whoever managed to dump Dyson here either had great planning skills or some help. Maybe both."

"Ugh. A very premeditated body dump. But why poor

Gladys?"

"She's a member of the Society, but new. So the body would be found and reported and she wouldn't easily be able to defend herself."

I snorted. "Like I would let the lions eat her."

"Like you'd have much say in her fate. *You're* new to the Society. And while I know you and some of your capabilities, I suspect that the general consensus is that you're a fluffy bunny."

"What is it with the fluffy bunny stuff? Just because blood turns my stomach, I'm a tiny prey animal?"

"And you don't have the enhanced characteristics of a vampire: speed, agility, strength, stamina. Not to mention the other enhancements that vary by individual."

"Ah, about that—" I flinched. I could have sworn I caught movement out of the corner of my eye. I peered cautiously over my shoulder, but Dyson wasn't moving. It looked like he was dead as dead could be.

"He's not moving. It's your imagination." Alex glanced at me with a small smile. "Or you've been sipping coffee on the sly and are hallucinating."

"Coffee doesn't make me hallucinate. See, there are some advantages to my less-vampiness."

"It's true, you do have a higher tolerance for coffee and caffeine—but you still have to watch it."

I tried to grab on to the mental thread of our previous conversation, but it kept slipping away. "What were we talking about?"

Alex got on the freeway. "Vampiric enhancements of the variable type."

"Oh, yes. Couldn't all of these weird little quirky things that you say resemble witch magic just be my own variety of vampire enhancements?"

"Except vampires get super speed—like your progenitor. Or stronger persuasion skills. Or an ability to fade into the background. Things that help them hunt."

I frowned. I didn't need to hunt, because I didn't drink blood.

"Uh, are we heading out of town?" Because that was definitely the Austin city limits sign we'd just passed.

"Buda, small town just south of Austin."

At the mention of our target destination, I glanced again over my shoulder. Still just a vaguely human-shaped lump, unmoving. "I know where Buda is. I didn't realize your source was outside of Austin."

"Barely."

"Humph." I'd been a downtown girl until very recently. As far as I was concerned, the burbs were in the sticks, so Buda was practically a foreign land. "What's up with this Star lady?"

"What do you mean?"

"How did you get hooked up with a medical examiner? Do you bribe her or what? Or is she also an enforcer, emergency responder person? Is she even a Society member? What's the scoop?"

"She's not an emergency responder. She's a witch but not exactly a member of the Society. I don't bribe her; I pay her a reasonable fee for her services." He pulled off the freeway and onto the frontage road. "She's an ex...I don't know—not really a girlfriend. She's an ex. Oh, and she's not a medical examiner. She's a mortician."

And he slowed down as we approached the sign for a funeral home. Then he turned and pulled into a long drive that led to a business.

A funeral home. A mortician. Because that wasn't creepy. Not at all.

11

STAR DOESN'T SHINE AT NIGHT

I wasn't sure what I expected. Nose rings, purple hair, lots of piercings? Maybe in the back of my brain. I hadn't really given it a lot of thought. And as important as witches were to the running of the Society, I'd yet to actually meet one in person. I knew they created stasis bottles to store blood for vamp consumption. And they were used to determine the veracity of a criminal's confession. There were all sorts of other things witches did that were a regular part of the Society's everyday life, but they eluded me in the moment.

Regardless of the fact that I didn't know what to expect, I knew Star wasn't it.

Five foot nothing, light blonde hair pulled back into a ponytail, no makeup—not that she needed it—and vibrating energy. The woman tapping her toe impatiently in front of the funeral home looked like she was absolutely a night person. Vibrant. Exuding energy. And peeved. I looked at the dash clock on the Volvo. We were all of fifteen minutes late. In the larger scheme of things, that wasn't so bad.

She approached the driver's-side window and, when Alex rolled it down, said, "Two a.m., you said. I won't be late, you said. This is the last time, you said." She crossed her arms, and from the slight bounce to her shoulders, I could tell that toe was still tapping. "Well, let me tell you, this is certainly the last time."

Alex blinked and then uttered one phrase that changed the woman's entire demeanor: "College fund."

Star turned to me and gave me a brilliant smile. "You're Alex's new friend Mallory."

I nodded, wide-eyed, unsure what exactly "Alex's new friend" implied, but hesitant to set her off again.

"All right. Pull around to the back, and I'll meet you there." Then she walked off with a purposeful, brisk gait.

"Not what I expected," I said after Alex had rolled up the window.

Alex shrugged. "She's a force of nature."

"And your former girlfriend."

He frowned. "Not exactly."

"Ew. Is that your less-than-subtle way of saying friends with benefits?"

He just shrugged. "Whatever we were, we're business acquaintances now. She's very married."

I was about to ask how a person could be "very" married when he said, "Four kids."

"Oh. And they're all little witches?"

"No. Witches are made, remember? Star is married to a normal human, and mostly retired. She's also sensitive to being called a witch—even though she still occasionally practices to help out with the kids' education fund."

"I mean, four kids... That's a lot of college money." I tried to keep my eyes from bugging out, but that really was a lot of cash.

"Exactly. Which is why I tell her every time that it's the last time—but I'm pretty sure she'll keep taking the odd job, so long as I don't abuse the privilege." Alex backed into a spot near the rear door.

The door opened to reveal Star now covered up in an apron. She looked like a baker with her hair pulled back and her sparkling white apron. I wrinkled my nose at the unfortunate comparison.

I expected a gurney, but she was empty-handed. She motioned for us to hurry, so I stepped out of the Volvo. Alex was already at the back popping the hatch. I was considering how the three of us would get the package out of the back when the sheet-wrapped body lifted.

"Ack!" I stumbled back. But then I realized Dyson wasn't moving, he was being levitated several inches. My hand flew to my chest, where my heart thumped like crazy.

Alex looked unsurprised.

"A little warning, okay?" I said under my breath.

I stepped back and watched as Star made a pulling motion, as if she was grabbing at the air and tugging.

"Get the door, Alex." She backed up, bringing the floating body of Dyson with her. She walked backward, pulling Dyson along like a balloon on a string. It was unnerving.

Alex opened the door, and Star disappeared inside, the bobbing, floating Dyson directly behind her. I hurried to follow Alex inside, and tried to pretend none of this was super creeping me out. You'd think I'd have a decent tolerance for the weird; I lived with a really old vamp. But Wembley was hardly scary. And while Alex's spirits were definitely disturbing, I'd only ever seen the one. And I knew Alex.

By the time I made it inside, my features schooled into

some semblance of calm, the body was on a raised metal table.

Star had retrieved some large scissors from a smaller table and was about to cut through the sheeting. She paused and looked at me. She narrowed her eyes, leaned back, then forward. "I thought you were supposed to be a vamp."

She said it like an accusation.

"I am a vamp." I didn't want to be defensive about my lack of blood drinking. I mean—yay, me. But she was giving me a complex with her intent and disapproving scrutiny.

"Huh." She turned back to the sheet and started to snip.

She began at the feet and worked her way up to the head. Her movements were deft, and she was careful not to cut anything but the sheet.

Her competent, sure movements stopped and she hovered uncertainly near Dyson's head, then backed away. "No way, Alex. You. Did. Not." Her free hand went to her hips and she turned to glare at Alex.

He gave her a sheepish look. "You didn't ask."

Great. It was obvious that Star not only knew who Dyson was, but that Alex had failed to inform her he'd be the one arriving dead on her doorstep.

She stood there, fuming, one hand on her hip and the other waving those giant shears in the air.

"An extra thousand?" Alex said.

He didn't look overly concerned about the scissors, so I decided not to be either. Except she kept waving them.

"Fifteen hundred? Come on—what does it really change? You know I'm legit. I'll do everything I can to find the perpetrator."

"Like I care about that. That's Society business. I just don't want Cornelius interfering with my side income. Two thousand, and you make this right between Cornelius and me." She pointed the scissors at him. "And you submit to a binding guarantee."

Alex closed his eyes with a pained expression. "Done."

I didn't think it was the cash that had him worried—so it must have had something to do with her methods of ensuring his cooperation, the binding guarantee. Hm.

"All right, then." Star turned back to Dyson, all business once again. She folded the sheet back to reveal the perfectly preserved corpse of Reginald Dyson.

"Shouldn't he look"—I cocked my head—"less alive?"

Star had revealed his whole body, still clothed, thankfully, and the sheet now hung down over the edges of the table. "What—you expected decay? On a golem? Won't happen. The creation tattoos prevent decay."

I'd forgotten that Wembley mentioned they had tats. "Okay—but even his color is good." I tilted my head. "Huh, he really isn't half bad-looking, is he?"

Star raised her pale eyebrows. "They're usually very attractive—if you're into reanimated dead parts."

My nose wrinkled. "No thanks."

"Exactly." She started to strip Dyson's clothes off. As she tugged at his pants, she looked up. "A little help?"

My gaze shot to Alex.

He shook his head. "I dug him up."

I choked back a protest that he'd dug him up *mostly*. I'd been the lucky soul to hit his fleshy body with my shovel. Ick.

But I needed to get over my squeamishness, so I helped Star strip Dyson. I tried not to look; I really did. The man was not only dead, he was dead and made up of someone else's parts. More than one someone, as I understood it. But then we got his pants off, and I was immediately distracted. The man was exceptionally well endowed.

"A vamp that blushes. Hm—there's something off about you," Star said. Then she laughed. "It is disconcerting on a dead guy, but golems are usually well-equipped. They can basically pick their own physical attributes, or their parents can." She shrugged.

I focused my gaze over Star's right shoulder. I couldn't look at Dyson, and I wasn't up to making eye contact with anyone right now. "So what did he die of? Was he murdered?"

"Was there any doubt? He's a golem." Star started to walk around the corpse, her hands splayed, palms down, and about three or four inches over Dyson's corpse. "Huh." She lifted her hands and brushed them together, as if brushing off dirt.

Alex had moved closer as Star began to work. He now stood at my left elbow. "A golem can't be killed in most of the normal ways. They die if you detach the head—but otherwise, the body is just a vessel for the magic that animates them."

"Defacing the creation tattoos creates some problems for a golem." Star bent over the series of tattoos. "These look intact."

"So no hanging for criminal golems?" I wasn't sure where that question came from.

"Oh, yes." Star's response was downright chipper. "There's a witch's noose that will drain the magic from a golem body. Kills them deader than dead—and still technically a hanging. The Society does like a hanging."

I blinked at her. And this woman had four non-witchy children. Wow. I supposed she didn't talk about hangings much at home, though.

"Our CEO had his magical mojo drained." Star moved to his head. Pointing to his neck, she said, "Not via hanging.

See, no marks. Given the lack of ligature marks anywhere on his body, I'd say a witch's noose didn't do the draining."

I went through the pieces I knew. "The tattoos keep him from rotting, and this magic inside of him animates him. So the tattoos are intact—"

"Yes, I'm almost certain that's why there's no decomposition." Star waved her hand toward the naked body. "Although there wouldn't have been much in the time frame that he's been dead, there'd be some. Golems do tend to decompose faster than humans once the creation tattoos are damaged."

Alex leaned close to the body. "But if all of his magic had been drained, he wouldn't look this close to alive."

Star smiled and nodded. "Yes. That's a clue, for sure. If I had to guess—and I would be guessing—I'd say he was slowly drained. Open the tap, and all the magic flows out. You get much pastier skin, blue lips, et cetera."

Alex sighed. "But let the tap drip and you get a slower death. At some point, the magic falls below a level sufficient to sustain life."

"And leaving"—Star waved a hand at the corpse—"this. A near-alive version of Reginald Dyson."

Alex's eyes narrowed.

"Oh—you've got a theory, don't you?" I could see it on his face.

"I have a suspicion," Alex said. "And it doesn't bode well for Mrs. Dyson."

"Ah," Star said. "Yes, it's possible." Turning to me, she said, "The magic used to create offspring has to come from somewhere. So both parents contribute small amounts over a period of time, collecting and storing it for the eventual creation of their child."

My brain tried to wrap itself around the math of that.

"So you're saying that golems aren't just composed of the magic given them by their parents. They have to gain some of their own from somewhere...otherwise wouldn't subsequent generations have less and less magic and eventually fade away from existence?"

"Yes." As she spoke, she began to levitate Dyson's body. "Golems are living beings, and they do generate their own magic. Just like wizards." She glanced at Alex, but then turned her attention back to Dyson. "Or witches, once they've crossed that threshold. Or vamps after the transformation."

Dyson was now several inches above the table. Star flicked her wrist, and he turned over, butt cheeks now facing up. She lowered him gently back down to the table. Which was good—because his bits were dangling, and it was beyond distracting.

Once Dyson was again firmly planted on the table, I thought about what she'd said. Vamps went through a transformation. Golem bodies were imbued with the spark of magical life collected from both their parents, and witches apparently crossed some unknown threshold. All of us made rather than born, but in very different ways.

I pressed my lips together. I remembered Alex saying that Star didn't like to discuss her witchiness—so I wasn't going to say a word. Even if it was torture to keep quiet.

But then I was distracted by the tattoos. Below the waistline of even the most daring and briefest of briefs was a tiny row of symbols.

Star caught my gaze. "They're all intact. Not that I had any doubts, given the state of the body."

"So, any ideas as to how the magic was drained?" Alex asked.

"If you're asking me to confirm your hypothesis, you

know I can't." Star walked away and pulled out a plain sheet from a drawer. "I don't know the specifics of how golem children are created any more than you do. Not how the magic is gathered or how it's stored. But the state of the body, the fact he hasn't been completely drained of magic, means slow syphoning. So, your theory is possible." She threw the sheet over his body, and both disappeared.

Gone. Not there anymore.

"Whoa. What just happened?" My eyes were glued to the table, where I knew—with zero doubt—Dyson's naked bum had been displayed.

"Cold storage, metaphorically." Star gave Alex a curious look. "That was the agreement?"

"Yeah."

"Well, I wish you only moderate luck in resolving your case. A little delay means I rack up heftier storage fees." Her eyes twinkled with good humor. "Just kidding."

I looked at the tiny woman who didn't for an instant look liked she'd had four kids. "You have four kids. I'm sure you're not."

She winked at me. When she turned back to Alex, her demeanor changed. "I know how much you like your sleep, so I'm sure you'll appreciate the fact that I have to get up in..." She glanced at the clock on the wall. "Just over three hours. Pay up."

Alex pulled out his wallet and took out a folded check. "Got a pen?"

I blinked. "You take checks? For illegal magical autopsies?"

Star raised her eyebrows. "I take checks for the occasional consulting fee." She pulled a pen out of her apron and handed it to Alex.

Once she'd received the check, which included her fee

for the autopsy and a few days of prepaid storage, she removed her apron and held out her hands to Alex.

Alex's face blanked off all emotion, then, with some deliberation, he grasped her outstretched hands.

I waited—but nothing visible happened.

Several seconds later, they were still holding hands and a little wrinkle had appeared in between Star's eyes.

She suddenly let go of his hands and stepped away. "What have you been up to, Alex?"

He looked as confused as she did. "I honestly don't know."

"Hm." Her eyes narrowed and her glance flitted between the two of us. "Whatever you've done, the binding won't take. You better make this right with Cornelius."

I didn't have a clue what she thought I had to do with whatever stumbling block she'd encountered. I did my best to look innocent and fluffy-bunny-like. Right up until I remembered the sparkles that had accompanied the pinky swear Alex and I had made not so long ago. Maybe I accidentally did something weird?

Alex gave me a thoughtful look, but didn't comment. Instead, he turned to Star and said, "You know I'll sort out Cornelius. The binding just lets you sleep better at night."

"True." She pointed first at Alex and then at me. "Something is up with you two. And don't give me that wide-eyed innocent look. You're still a vamp, bloodsucking or not."

Which made me laugh. She shot me an annoyed look, so I explained, "I get a lot of fluffy bunny comments."

"Hm. I'm not sure exactly what's going on with you, but you're no fluffy bunny."

Which made me feel all warm inside, because I didn't feel like a fluffy bunny. I wasn't a bloodthirsty vamp predator, but that didn't make me a fluffy bunny. And those sparkles...well, someday I'd figure that out.

"All right. I'm tired and I have to get up in...well, now it's less than three hours. Get lost. My poor kids are going to have a hard enough time dealing with me tomorrow without me losing any more sleep." As we headed to the exit, she said, "Alex, be careful."

"Yeah." His response came out clipped, even borderline rude. But then he opened the door for me, and we left.

When I got in the wagon, I noticed a distinctly fresh scent. "Um, why does the car smell like lemons and sunshine?"

"That was part of the deal. She'd keep the corpse and clean the car." Alex pulled into the drive. "I can't return Gladys's car smelling like dirt and dead guy."

"Fair point. Is it just me, or do witches have the best magic?"

"Bite your tongue." He pulled out onto the frontage road.

Hm. Seemed like they were super handy—but I'd let it go for now. "We should talk about our suspect list."

"I was thinking about that. Since we don't know much about golem procreation, maybe it's not necessarily Ophelia Dyson. For all we know, it could be some other female golem."

"And we're sure it takes both a male and a female to create little baby golems?"

"Yes—but they're hardly little golems when they're created."

I skipped over that mental image as quickly as possible. "So the happy couple collect the necessary energy or magic somehow, then they use that for baby making. So who's to say there isn't another way to collect the magic energy stuff? Or maybe the normal method of energy collection was abused here. Except...you'd think Dyson would notice. I mean, his magic life juice was being slowly sucked away. How does a guy not notice that?"

"I have no idea. You'd think he'd be tired, feel under the weather, something."

"So we need to know more about how golems reproduce—"

"Humph. Not gonna happen."

I ignored that much too pessimistic and not at all helpful attitude. "And also if there's some way to suck the magic juice or life essence out of a guy other than sex or however golems do their baby making."

"Huh."

I looked at him, but he didn't elaborate. "Huh? What does 'huh' mean?"

Without taking his eyes of the road, he said, "Sex and draining energy—what does that make you think of?"

I trawled through the depths of my memory for a mythological match. "Succubus—but is that a thing?" Sexed to death, the best way to go or the worst? I couldn't help but go there. And I wasn't sure of the answer.

"Maybe. I mean, succubi aren't a class of enhanced being. But could such an enhancement exist? Sure."

I ticked off the must-dos on our sleuthing list. "Find out more about golem procreation—shush, we can at least try—dig around for alternative methods of collecting golem energy, and find out if we have any sneaky succubi hiding out in the Austin area."

"Basically all of those things are nearly impossible—maybe the alternatives for energy collecting—but the rest... First, golems are notoriously guarded about their procreation. Second, the Society maintains no record of the enhancements of each person, just the general class. Vamp, golem, witch, et cetera."

"You're speeding." I refrained from grasping at the door —barely.

"I'm annoyed."

"Well, you can definitely get a list of female golems, then. That's a start."

Alex slowed down as we approached an intersection. He flipped a U, and started back toward town. "Yep. Will do as soon as I get some rest."

I snuggled into the seat a little deeper. Yeah, a rested Alex was best for everyone. I really should find out what those spirit things could do to him if they caught him in a weakened state. It had to be pretty bad, otherwise why be so careful?

❧

"Mallory. Mallory. Mallory!"

"Ah! I'm up—what?" I blinked at an annoyed-looking Alex, who sat in the driver's seat of a car.

I looked around—I was in Gladys's Volvo. Which was parked in my driveway. And it was dark. Then I remembered: well-endowed dead body, witch mortician, succubi—

"You snore."

"Do not." I frowned at him and did a quick drool check.

"Okay. You're home."

He looked a little ragged around the edges, and I squinted at him, looking for any signs that those little wispy spirit boogers were flitting around or clinging to his neck. I couldn't see anything, but he definitely looked tired. "You wanna crash on the sofa?"

"I'll just sleep at the office tonight."

"Right—on the futon. Where do you live again?" I tried to remember what part of town his real place was—but now that I thought on it, I wasn't sure I knew. He seemed to practically live at his office. "Wait, you do have a home, don't you?"

His eyes crinkled in amusement. "I have a home. Out southwest, in Dripping Springs. It's more of a weekend place these days, and the traffic just gets worse every year—but the neighborhood is still pretty quiet."

I nodded. It was good he had a quiet place to hang out, recover, be himself. He seemed the kind of guy who could use that. I shook my head. "Right. You're probably ready to get to bed. Thanks for driving. What time is our appointment tomorrow—today—with Mrs. Dyson?"

"Not till two. Get some rest. I'll pull the other golem names from the rolls, and you can have a look on the way. The rest...well, we'll chat about the rest tomorrow. Get some sleep tonight." I got out and was about to close the door when he added, "But set your alarm and turn up the volume."

I saluted him and moved my tired rear in the direction of the front door. I was walking into the house before I heard the Volvo reverse out of the drive.

"What took you so long? What happened?" Wembley met me in the entryway. He was wearing a brown velour robe that had seen better days, but at least it was snugly tied.

"You really have lost some weight." I needed to quit commenting on it or the guy would get a complex, but I was tired and the filter between my brain and my mouth was sketchy.

"Been training. I told you that. What happened?"

"Right. Um, basically? He had his magic life juice sucked out."

Wembley crossed his arms. "Those were not Star's words."

"I can't remember, and I'm tired." The words came out whinier than I would have liked. But I *was* tired. I straightened. "Wait. Do you know Star?"

"Quick whiskey in the kitchen?"

I didn't hesitate, just turned on my heel and headed to the kitchen. I'd discovered a bottle of Johnny Walker Black stashed in the back of a cupboard at my old place when I'd been having a pretty rough day. I'd given it a try, and discovered that vamp-me liked the stuff. I'd never been much of a whiskey drinker before my transformation.

I poured us both a decent-sized glass of Macallan. Why not? The stuff tasted great, and as vamps we had a better tolerance than most. Well, I did. Wembley went a little further than a "better tolerance." He could drink a bottle of the stuff without pause, and you'd never know he'd had a sip but the fumes. It was downright freakish.

"So," I said, placing the glass in front of him on the kitchen table. "Spill."

"She was active in the Society but left to settle down out in the country. We don't have many witches as powerful as Star—but the appeal of children and a normal life was greater than the pull of witchy power." Wembley took a swig of his whiskey. "And that's saying something. It's a powerful pull. Even an addiction for some. But children and a 'normal' life were more important for her."

I sat kitty-corner to him. "Yeah, she seems pretty focused on the kids. She was only helping to build up their college fund—or so I gathered."

"That might be part of the reason. But magic—the power the witch gains as she acquires new spells, the rush of using them—can be addictive. I bet she does these little favors for Alex in part for the cash, but also for the sheer pleasure of it."

"Maybe." But I wasn't sure I bought it. She seemed more like a super mom than an addict. But what did I know about magic? I had a thimble's worth of knowledge. And speaking of, now seemed a prime time to ask about my weird, not-quite vampy powers.

"You know they were an item."

My head popped up. "Huh?"

"Alex and Star." Wembley took a drink, but he was watching me over the top of the glass.

"So?" Alex had said as much—but Wembley made it sound more than a fling.

He shrugged. "Just thought you'd be interested. Did Alex or Star have any thoughts on who might have been able to deplete Dyson's magic? Or how they did it?"

I was still considering what exactly an "item" was—especially since Alex claimed she hadn't been his girlfriend. And I'd gotten the distinct impression they were shag buddies.

"Hello?" Wembley his hand in front of my face.

"Sorry, you wanted to know how? They weren't sure, though they guessed it was slow, which made Alex wonder if it was some kind of lady golem thing. I guess when a golem couple has a kid, they collect their magical energy over time." I scrunched my nose up. "I guess I should be all about the magical miracle of birth—but it's all a little..."

"Humph. Golem parents can coo over the miracle of their offspring's creation, but we can agree it's not a particularly appealing aspect of their magic."

I sniggered. "Says the guy who drinks blood."

"Says the puny vamp." Wembley arched an eyebrow.

"True enough." My jaw cracked with a massive yawn. "And I think I need more sleep than you." I finished off the last of my Macallan and stood up to go, but I couldn't help asking, "What exactly do you mean that Alex and Star were an item?"

"Ah, they lived together for a few years, back before she went straight and reproduced."

I coughed whiskey fumes. "I'm sorry—what?"

"Out in Dripping Springs; they had a little place with goats and a mule or two." Wembley gave me a knowing look. "You okay?"

I nodded and waved him off, but the booze vapor was still in my nose when I got to my bedroom.

12

MIRROR IMAGE

Alex was in a rotten mood, and I wasn't even to blame. I'd woken to my alarm around noon—the first time that I could remember since becoming a vamp—and been ready to go when he swung by to pick me up an hour later.

My promptness hadn't made a dent in his foul mood. And when I asked if everything was okay, he'd snapped at me—so we'd driven in silence.

He parked the car in the drive and ran his hand through his hair. "Sorry. I didn't sleep well last night." His gaze remained firmly fixed in the distance. "Nightmares."

I could only imagine what kind of nightmares a man like Alex had. "I'm sorry. Have the spirits been bothering you?"

He closed his eyes and shook his head. "No." He turned and looked at me. "I just wanted to tell you I'm sorry for letting it interfere with our work."

"Hey, we're here on time. No interference."

"Right. You know what I mean." He didn't wait for me to respond, just exited the car.

I scrambled to catch up. A few steps before he reached the door, I said, "Do you have a plan?"

"Mostly just get a feel for both of them. I only know Rachael." He rapped sharply on the door. "I've never met Ophelia, Mrs. Dyson. Like I said before, we don't run in the same circles."

I still didn't understand how that could be possible. The Society seemed like a really small community.

The door opened to reveal Gladys. Or a woman that could have been Gladys's twin. Tall, fiery red hair that was almost the exact shade of Gladys's, perfect pale skin. Even the nose and shape of the eyes... Whoa.

The Gladys copy gave me a curious look then looked down at herself. "I'm sorry—not what you expected?"

I shut my gaping mouth.

Alex said, "You bear a striking resemblance to an acquaintance. Mallory isn't normally so rude...or so silent."

"Right, sorry." I was so flustered that I stuck out my hand, temporarily forgetting that enhanced humans weren't usually into handshakes.

I realized my mistake and was withdrawing my hand when Ophelia shook it. A firm, solid shake. Quite professional, in fact. Not what I expected from a shopaholic wearing a flowing dress that emphasized rather than hid all of her curves. But I also really needed to stop judging people based on their grip. Maybe also not on their appearance—though there usually were a few good tells in a person's choice of clothing and hair style. Ophelia Dyson had beautiful taste and knew how to dress to make herself look even more gorgeous.

She gave me a sly smile. "Not a problem for golems. Ophelia Dyson. You're here about my husband's very inconvenient disappearance?" Withdrawing her hand, she opened the door wider, gesturing for us to come inside.

The creepy sense of being in the presence of Gladys-but-not-Gladys faded with each passing second. Gladys was many things, but not sly. And her manner was open and genuine, unlike the calculated perfection of Ophelia Dyson.

"Is there a particular reason that now is inconvenient?" Alex asked.

Ophelia led the way to a large room that looked like it belonged inside a private club more than a home. Small groupings of furniture were clustered throughout the room. She indicated a loveseat and two chairs around a coffee table, where a coffee set was laid out. A small trickle of steam floated out and away from the silver spout.

Once we'd seated ourselves, she said, "Any unexplained absence is inconvenient. What does one say? Fake an illness? Give no explanation? Worse—tell the truth? Add to that the mundane policing force..." She shook her head. "Very inconvenient." Gesturing to the table, she said, "May I offer you coffee?"

She only looked a little surprised when I accepted. Either she thought I liked to conduct interviews high, or some of my less vamp-like peculiarities were circulating.

"Have you spoken with the police?" I asked. I didn't particularly relish any interaction with the police in my capacity as sleuthing vamp. I'd grown up in the mundane community. I was conditioned to respect and even fear police. I didn't particularly want to run afoul of the local cops.

"Oh, no. We've managed to avoid that thus far. Reginald worked primarily from his home office. We can likely delay any outsiders noticing his absence for at least another week. But eventually, notice will be taken." Ophelia raised her eyebrows. "My hope is that you'll dig him up before that happens."

I almost choked on my scalding hot, velvety delicious, premium coffee.

Ophelia gave me a politely curious look.

"Very hot. Sorry," I said sheepishly. Because the woman couldn't have any idea we'd literally been digging her husband up the night before. Could she?

I looked at Alex, but his gaze slid away before I could get a read on what he was thinking.

"Perhaps you can share your husband's calendar with us." Alex sipped his coffee slowly, cupping the delicate china in his hands, rather than holding it by the ridiculously small handle.

Delicately arched brows climbed. "I understood that you'd received his schedule from his assistant, Becky Taylor. We're quite friendly, you know. She lives in the guesthouse." She pointed over her shoulder at the massive picture windows on the backside of the room. "Just there."

"So she keeps not only his professional calendar but also his personal and social schedules?"

Ophelia replaced her cup in its saucer after a ladylike sip. "Yes, that's correct. Reginald and I don't particularly get along these days." She leaned slightly forward. "I don't suppose that he's dead, and his body disposed of in some nefarious and difficult-to-find way?"

Alex started to reply, but Ophelia waved her hand. "No, it's quite all right. I know you can't answer that. It's just wishful thinking that the horrible man has passed on. I mean, he's a golem. We're terribly difficult to kill." Turning to me, she said, "You may not be aware, but golems are a hardy bunch."

"So it would be *good* if your husband was dead?" I spoke tentatively, because the question seemed beyond gauche. But she'd started the thread...

"Oh, lovely. But only if he were dead. Missing isn't at all helpful. Like I said, so inconvenient."

I considered the advantages and disadvantages to Ophelia's disclosure. I mean, what murderer said outright that they'd be thrilled if the dead guy was dead?

But Dyson wasn't publicly dead. So far as anyone knew, he was missing. But then again, the connection between Gladys and myself was hardly a secret, and, likewise, the connection between Alex and myself wasn't a secret. Hm. She could know that Alex and I knew about her husband's death and that we knew where the body was... I looked up to find Alex and Ophelia deep in conversation about Dyson's investments.

Oops. That might be important.

"So generally healthy?" Alex asked.

"Oh, yes. I spend cash to upset him. He's quite boringly and respectably flush." Ophelia grinned. "His death would free up at least my portion of the estate. Texas and its lovely community property laws—so helpful in these situations."

"So his disappearance doesn't free up those funds in a similar way?" I asked. I was fuzzy on legalities. I'd never been married, so familiarizing myself with marital property laws wasn't high on my to-do list.

"Oh, no. The exact opposite. Most of the funds are in his name, which makes access tricky. An intentional act on his part, and certainly one I can circumvent in a prolonged absence, but it will be inconvenient." She leaned forward conspiratorially. "I may have to curb my spending for a short period."

She didn't look particularly put out at the thought. Maybe she really did only spend to make her husband mad. Bizarre. What married people did to each other during marital disputes boggled the mind. And also seemed to stretch across the mundane and magical lines.

"He doesn't seem to have any social or financial enemies of significant note," Alex said. Thankfully—because I'd missed that entire conversation as I speculated on the depth of Ophelia's knowledge and whether her digging comment had been intentional, a slip of the tongue, or coincidence.

"That I know of," Ophelia interjected. "As I said, Becky is much more involved with his schedule. And his work and political lives, naturally."

My ears perked up. "Is there a difference? I thought Mr. Dyson, Reginald, spent most of his time managing the Society."

"Ah. That position doesn't actually pay much, dear." Ophelia lifted the pot with a questioning look, but Alex and I declined.

Odd. I had the impression that the Society was well funded. I swallowed the cold dregs of my coffee and considered what that meant.

Alex took pity and explained. "The wages were frozen in the eighties and no one has bothered to change them since. Most of the members who hold positions within the Society have personal wealth that makes the Society salary negligible."

"So what's his profession?" I asked. How was a girl to keep track of motives when Dyson's life just kept getting more complicated? Then again, I was pretty sure Ophelia was guilty as heck.

But I'd thought that about Becky, too.

And for just the blink of an eye, Gladys.

And Rachael, who I'd never even met, but was noticeably absent today.

Hm...

"Oil and gas, but he dabbles in IT and some other things." Ophelia lifted her hands like it was all too much to keep up with.

I had to bite back a laugh. I'd bet dollars to dimes that Ophelia knew not only exactly how Dyson spent his time, but that she also knew—give or take a few hundred thousand—what the guy was worth at any given moment.

Alex frowned at me. "Just to recap, you're not aware of any recent business dealings that would have caused your husband difficulties?"

"No. Nor social commitments, nor political intrigues." Ophelia's previously perfect posture melted, and she leaned back in her chair. "The man is incredibly boring. In every facet of his life. Even his women..." She waved a hand.

My eyeballs practically bugged out, but I bit my tongue.

Alex jumped in, with no indication of discomfort or embarrassment. "What can you tell us about his extramarital relationships?"

"The man had a type, and I'm it." A small smile played about her mouth when her gaze landed on mine. "Tall, slender but busty, and red-red hair. Ah—and no freckles. He found them vulgar."

"Is there anything else that you can think of that might help us locate him?" Alex asked. "A favorite vacationing spot? A friend or relative he'd spoken of visiting?"

"I think we all know the man is dead." Ophelia rose from her chair with an air of casual elegance. If I didn't know what she was, I'd guess she'd been a dancer at some point. Maybe she had some poor dancer's body. Who knew. I stood up quickly, appalled at the direction of my thoughts.

Then her words sank in.

"Oh, but there's no way to be sure..." My words petered

off as I realized that of course there was. I *was* sure, because I'd seen his dead body.

"No," she said as she escorted us to the front. "I'm sure he is. But it would be lovely if you could recover his body. Or failing that, perhaps some definitive and legally admissible evidence of his demise? I suppose I can wait the seven years, but it's all so inconvenient."

I stood on her front steps and tried to digest her words. They came from a woman who lived in a different universe from my own.

"Very inconvenient," Alex said.

I turned to Alex. He was just as bad.

"There's a hefty bonus for you should you manage that body—or the admissible evidence." She gave Alex a warm smile.

I shifted my gaze from one to the other. I was in the land of crazy. And we hadn't even met the daughter. No telling what she was like. The daughter... "Is your daughter Rachael included in his will?"

"Oh yes. She inherits everything. After the community property is split, of course. But Rachael wouldn't harm a hair on her dear papa's head. She's almost as devoted to him as dear Becky. Best not mention his likely death to Becky. The poor woman will be devastated, and I really can't deal with that right now. Better to leave her in an indefinite state of denial. Do let me know what you find, and don't forget that bonus." With a polite but dismissive smile, she said, "Goodbye," and shut the door.

I didn't realize I was staring at the closed door until I felt Alex's hand at my elbow, gently guiding me away. "Wow. Just wow."

Alex didn't reply. In fact, he tugged on my arm a little less gently.

I took the hint and headed for the car. As soon as I closed the door, I said, "Well, she did it."

"Why? Because you don't like her?"

I thumped Alex in the arm. "Were you listening? She said that she wants him dead. She offered us a bribe to return the body. Or am I confused? How much guiltier could she be?"

"Were *you* listening?" Alex rubbed his arm—as if a little flick would hurt. "Dyson had a thing for Gladys-lookalikes. Or, more accurately, Mrs. Ophelia Dyson lookalikes. So we have to consider the other red-haired women Dyson was likely screwing. We also have to consider that he might have been screwing one particular red-head, as you don't want to think about—"

"Don't say Gladys." I snapped my seatbelt in place as Alex pulled out of the drive. "That will just make me sad. I mean, I have my own doubts, but they're tiny doubts. What you're talking about—that she was his lover—would be a huge departure from the truth as I understand it."

"Would it? If Gladys is overcoming her issues with men, then maybe she was attracted to Dyson. They had sex, she regretted it—or maybe even was frightened at some point—and bam..."

"Seriously? And bam? She all of sudden sucks the life from him, just like that?"

"Agreed. That doesn't jibe with the facts. And, of course, I just don't see Gladys pulling this off. I never have."

"Whew. Thank goodness. Glad I'm not the only one who thinks premeditation is a step too far for Gladys. And however he died, Dyson *was* killed with some planning. Maybe—and that's one huge, hard to overcome maybe—she could do some damage in a passionate, overwrought moment like you just described, but no way she could or would plan his death."

"And then there's the question of motive."

I snapped my fingers. "Right. If you rule out conflicted passion and guilt and all those other complicated feelings we have when we sleep with the wrong guy, then where's the motive?"

Alex choked.

"What?"

"You sleep with the wrong guys a lot?"

I rolled my eyes. A woman would get it. "I'm telling you: it's Ophelia. That woman has premeditated murder oozing from her pores." I gave that a little thought. "Or Rachael. She could have been hiding out to keep us from spotting her guilt."

"Or for some other reason." But Alex didn't elaborate on what particular reasons he had in mind. "And again, you're overlooking the obvious. Dyson's other women."

"Ah yes. Them. That would explain the spirits' comment. Looks like Gladys, but isn't Gladys. And actually, the spirits' evidence really does work nicely to implicate Ophelia, too. Except how would a Gladys lookalike, whether Ophelia or some other red-headed woman, end up at Gladys's house with Dyson?"

"She was planned as the patsy all along."

"I suppose." I couldn't help thinking: why poor Gladys, of all people? Then I had a really gross thought. "Do golem children ever resemble their parents?"

Alex whizzed around a corner a little too fast for my comfort, and I grabbed hold of the seat.

"Sorry," he said, and slowed down a little. "No, Rachael doesn't look like her mother. Dark hair and not as tall."

"Well, the only red-headed women we have so far are

Gladys and Ophelia, and I have to say again that Ophelia is looking good for it."

"Where's the proof?"

Proof would be good...or rather imperative, given the inner workings of the Society's justice system. It was ragged around the edges, at best. Downright inquisitional on a bad day. So not just proof, but proof such that no doubt could possibly exist. Really awesome, exceptional, irrefutable proof. "Right. What about that list of golem women?"

"Very short. Only a handful of names, and no red-heads —not natural, anyway. But you forget, the only evidence we have that the murderer was red-headed are a few confused spirits. Confused and hazy spirits aren't the type of evidence I'd like to rely on, and it's not something I can present to Cornelius."

"That is shady— Uh, sorry. No pun intended." I did sometimes get punny when I was stressed out. But he'd started it with the "hazy" nonsense. Stress-induced pun usage was certainly one of the less attractive traits I'd gained as a vamp.

"I think we need to stick to the one solid piece of evidence that we have," Alex said.

I groaned. "But that's only one tiny piece of info: Dyson's magic life essence was slowly sucked away. We don't know how, or even why that particular method was chosen. It seems so haphazard."

Alex switched lanes and shot me a quick glance. "We need more evidence."

"Buzzkill." But he was right. Much as my gut said Ophelia, or Rachael—maybe Becky—we needed evidence. Yeah, we really needed some evidence.

Alex just grinned. "That's better than killing your happy."

"Oh no, you're doing that—with your buzzkill ways." I sighed. "Okay, you're not really. You are a buzzkill, but my happy is alive and well. Sleuthing is fun, especially when the stakes are a little less personal."

I was pretty sure Alex groaned, but it could also have been some noise from the radio that I'd just flipped on.

13

ILLEGAL VAMPIRING?

I'd remembered to update my calendar, and as Alex and I were headed back into town, I got a reminder about an appointment with my decorator.

"But I can totally skip it," I said after Alex asked what was up.

I might have sounded a little too eager, because he said, "You don't want Wembley to finish, do you?"

I scowled back at him. To admit that was to admit I was a lonely, sad, pathetic soul. Blech.

"Come on. What's the big deal, Mallory? Just tell him. He'd probably be thrilled to room with you. Especially if you let him keep the master bedroom. He doesn't need to live in his half-finished houses; he just doesn't like living alone. All the contractor noise and motion makes him feel like he's not."

"Hmph." Pathetic. Sad. Lonely. No thanks.

"Whatever. Just think about it." Alex tensed, and I followed his laser-like focus to a car parked in front of my house.

One that looked suspiciously like an unmarked cop car.

"Maybe you should just keep driving," I said, motioning with my hand off to the right, where another residential street intersected with mine.

He ignored me and pulled into my driveway. "Bad idea. But I am going in with you."

I felt some of the tension in my chest ease. Which made no sense. What could Alex do if the cops wanted me. "Ah—why am I freaking out? I haven't actually done anything wrong."

"Because the cops are at your house." He said it so matter-of-factly that I felt less crazy for feeling panicked.

"I'm a vegan, for goodness' sake. It's not like I'm out assaulting people's necks for sustenance." I looked at Alex, then the front door, then Alex. "Wembley..." I hopped out of the car and headed to the door quickly as I could. Which actually turned out to be pretty fast. I blinked back at Alex, who was several steps behind me. "Was that as fast as—"

"A normal vamp. I'd say yes."

Huh—but no time for that. I threw open the front door and hollered, "Wembley!"

"In the kitchen, heathen." He emerged into the living room, looking not one bit flustered. "You have company, so put on your nice manners and use your inside voice."

"*I* have company?" I walked into the kitchen on Wembley's heels to find a man sitting at the table with a half-drunk cup of coffee in front of him.

Alex wrapped a proprietary arm around my shoulders and kissed my cheek. In a barely perceptible whisper, he said, "Breathe."

And I exhaled the breath I'd been holding for several seconds. Then I smiled. And then everything was fine. Whatever this cop wanted, he wasn't here to haul me off for illegal vampirism. And that was just silly enough for me to smile.

I stepped forward and offered my hand.

Wembley said, "Mallory, Detective Ruiz. Detective Ruiz, this is Mallory Andrews."

The detective stood to shake my hand, and I had one of those girly double-take moments. How had I missed how obscenely attractive this guy was? Even for a few seconds? Built, really built—like hours-in-the-gym-every-day built. Not tall, but tall enough to top me by a few inches even with heels on. As if I'd wear heels. Inky-black hair that begged to be rumpled. Melty brown eyes. He was delicious.

As my eyes slid up and down as discreetly as possible, I landed on the badge attached to his belt. Aha, that was why I hadn't noticed his utter hotness right away.

"Ms. Andrews. I didn't have a good number for you, but this address is listed as your current residence. I'd like to ask you a few questions, if you have a moment." Detective Ruiz glanced at Alex.

Alex seated himself at the table as if he'd been invited.

I gestured for the detective to have a seat again and sat down opposite him.

Wembley presented me with a fresh cup of coffee, and then sat next to me. I looked at the coffee and then Wembley. Was he trying to get me coffee-high? Although he couldn't know about that cup I'd had earlier...could he? Hm. He did have a mischievous glint to his eye.

I turned away from him and said to the detective with a politely firm tone, "What can I help you with?"

He took out a pad and pen. "I understand that you were neighbors with Mrs. Arbuthnot before her death."

My eyes started to burn. It wasn't like I cried every time I thought of her. And she certainly wouldn't have approved if

I did. It just surprised me. It was the last thing I expected him to ask about. I mean, Dyson's dead body was...somewhere. And Alex and I were in the midst of a murder investigation. Mrs. A and her technically unsolved murder weren't at the top of my brain. Mostly because it *was* solved. And my nice-old-lady-killing progenitor had fried for her murder. Well, according to the Society's rules of execution, he'd actually hung—but either way, he was super dead.

A pristine white hanky appeared in front of me. I looked up into Alex's concerned face. When I didn't take it right away, he said, "Please."

Then I remembered—my poisonous tears—and dabbed at the corners of my eyes. What had Alex called them? Bitter tears? More like acid than something just bitter, they left red streaks on my face if I let them run unchecked. I dabbed again. Tears that burned my face would be really hard to explain to Detective Ruiz.

"Sorry," I said, crumpling the hanky in my fist. "She was a friend, and I didn't know that's what you'd be asking about."

Detective Ruiz looked up from his pad with curiosity.

Oops. *Don't mention the dead guy. Don't mention the dead guy. Don't—*

"Is there something else you'd expect me to ask you about?"

Don't mention the dead guy. I shook my head. "No."

I had to hold my spine rigid, because I wanted to slump in relief. I was sick of my mouth taking off without my full cooperation. The extra effort I was exerting to keep my thoughts to myself these days was tiring.

"You know that we're investigating Mrs. Arbuthnot's death as suspicious?"

"I didn't, but I'm glad to hear it." Except that was a fat lie.

I absolutely knew that an investigation had begun. Because I'd had Bradley poke around, and he dug up the open investigation. "I would hate for anyone to think that she'd killed herself. She would never have done that."

"There is evidence to support an alternative explanation for her death," Detective Ruiz said.

Alex shifted in his seat, drawing all eyes to him. "What evidence?"

Detective Ruiz's jaw firmed. He did not like Alex. Interesting, because women adored him. The detective said, "Nothing we can share. It's an open case."

Alex's expression didn't change, but the room felt tenser. "What do you want from Mallory? You can see speaking about Mrs. A is upsetting for her."

"And you are?" the detective asked with pen poised over pad.

"Alex Valois." Alex gave him a mildly amused look. "I have my license if you'd like to see it. V-a-l-o-i-s."

The detective shook his head. "That's fine. Did you also know Angela Arbuthnot—Mrs. A?"

"Unfortunately, no. Mallory and I got together after Mrs. A passed."

I shot him a warning look, but he wouldn't meet my eyes. I had no clue why he was implying that we were an item, but it was annoying. Especially given the fact that he'd never once looked at me like I was on his dating—or even casual sex—radar. I'd have noticed; I wasn't that oblivious.

I considered for a second whether I had a chance with the hot detective, then decided that a vamp and a cop would be a catastrophe waiting to happen. Decision made, I turned to Alex and gave him a sickly sweet smile. "It was an amazing first meeting. Practically love at first sight, wasn't it, sweetie?"

Alex just nodded agreeably. "If you say so."

The man was annoyingly unflappable. I asked Detective Ruiz, "Is there anything that you can share with us? Are you making any progress?"

No way he could be making that much progress, what with the killer no longer on the face of the planet. The vile rat had been summarily hung and his body disposed of in some way I was sure meant he'd never be found. The Society was good at that sort of hush-hush, top-secret stuff. So imagine my surprise when the detective replied that yes, progress was being made.

Liar, liar, pants on fire. I hoped. That, or the Society was in danger of some close police scrutiny.

"Can you tell me if she had any visitors that week?" the detective asked.

Bradley would know—but I wasn't about to sic the police on poor Bradley. "Well, Mrs. A was pretty social. She got along with all of the neighbors really well. Anyone from the floor certainly could have visited."

"But what about other visitors, someone not from the building? Like a relative or a delivery service."

"Well..." I considered if she had family, but couldn't recall any. "No family that I know of—but I wouldn't necessarily. I can tell you that she didn't do fast food, and she fetched her own groceries. She didn't believe in all of the little conveniences that kept people separated from each other. And she had strong feelings about walking. She walked to the small boutique grocery around the corner every week, and she made a trip to the larger store once a month."

"She sounds like a lady who had very definite opinions."

I smiled. "She was, but not in that stagnant, refusing-to-change way that some people have. She wanted the people around her to be healthy and happy. I think she had a really full life filled with loving people. Her husband did die young, and that was a terrible blow for her—but she wasn't bitter or resentful." I started to get teary again. I'd never really considered it one way or another. She really had been an interfering, nosy busybody with a heart of gold. Sometimes annoying, but always with the best of intentions.

I dabbed at my eyes. They had to be all sorts of pink by now.

"We suspect that someone mixed the hydrocodone in a drink and forced her to swallow it." Detective Ruiz frowned. Maybe he regretted saying so much.

I wadded up the hanky and looked into Detective Ruiz's eyes. "I hope you have fingerprints or some kind of evidence, because Mrs. A's killer shouldn't get away with her murder."

And he hadn't, the nasty, neck-raping perv. But poor Detective Ruiz didn't know that, couldn't know that, and if he did find out...well, that would create some serious problems for him.

"We're actively working on her case. Can you give me an email address and phone number where I can reach you with further questions?"

"Certainly," I said, and rattled off my contact information.

Wembley, who'd been intently watching but silent through the brief exchange, said, "Will you update Mallory when you close the case? Since she was so close to Mrs. A, I'm sure it would be a relief to know when the killer is caught."

I blinked then added, "Yes. That would be a great relief."

Detective Ruiz closed his notebook calmly and placed it

and his pen in his pocket. "I'll see what I can do." He stood up and thanked us for our time before leaving.

After I'd closed the door on him and watched him get in his car through the peephole, I turned to find Wembley and Alex both hovering directly behind me.

"Weird, right?" I asked them.

"Yes," both answered simultaneously.

Wembley headed back to the kitchen, and Alex and I followed along.

"Why come here?" I asked Wembley's retreating back. "I guarantee that the police have a way to get my cell phone number. They have to, right?"

"Yes." Wembley waited until we were all back in the kitchen, and said, "He wanted to meet you, see how you reacted. Whiskey?"

I nodded. It was never too early for a whiskey—not since I stopped getting a buzz. Three cheers for the vamp virus, because I liked whiskey and didn't love the feeling of having drunk too much.

Alex declined with a shake of his head. "Now that the autopsy has confirmed foul play, of course there's an investigation." He pinned me with an intent look. "But Mrs. A's killer has already met a just end, so we're not really concerned about him. We need to be more worried about keeping the police out of the current investigation into Dyson's death—or, rather, his disappearance."

"Hey, I don't want people to think she killed herself. Not only was she not prone to suicidal tendencies, but *she didn't actually kill herself*." I returned his stare. "Sometimes you guys need to think about the little people."

Wembley snorted.

"What?" I asked.

"There is so much wrong with that. First, you're a part of

the Society. You're one of the bad enhanced humans, remember?" Wembley smirked. "And the little people? Even I don't think of mundanes as the little people."

I winced. I hadn't meant it that way—not consciously. But instead of explaining myself, I took a page from Tangwystl's book and blew a raspberry at him.

"Nice. Very mature," Wembley said, but he was smiling.

"Hey, focus on the bigger picture." Alex turned to Wembley. "I will take a small one."

I narrowed my gaze. "Should you—"

"Don't." That was all Alex said, and not in a mean tone, but it was enough.

"Sorry."

And I was. Alex knew better than anyone else exactly what was and wasn't okay. He'd lived with his own personal demons for...well, probably a long time now. I wasn't sure what I was thinking. "Maybe that cop flustered me more than I realized."

Wembley delivered a glass with a long pour to me and a short pour to Alex then retrieved his own. "To solving Dyson's death."

We raised our glasses. We could all drink to that.

I leaned back against the counter and said, "What's next?"

"We check out the golems listed on the Society's rolls," Alex said.

"Ugh." I turned to Wembley. "We have a rather suspect lead that points to a red-headed woman. I think it's got to have some merit, but Alex is suspicious."

"I am, but we'll still minimally investigate the red-headed golem population. All I'm saying is that the lead needs some context. Which means—"

"We need more proof." I wrinkled my nose. "Finding

Dyson's killer and clearing Gladys is a lot harder than I envisioned it being."

Wembley choked on a laugh. "That's because the last murderer found *you*."

"Watch it, buddy." I tipped my glass at him. "You're the one he caught unawares and conked on the head."

"True—but I'm not going around trying to solve murders and thinking it's all a game. I'm also in training again, so there shouldn't be a repeat incident." Wembley stood up a little straighter and patted his formerly quite paunchy midsection. "It was past time."

I pinched my lips together. "Okay. How do we check out the golem women?"

Alex grinned. "I had an idea about that. Do you think your friend Bradley could pull their credit card transactions and check for alibis?"

"Um—sure? But alibis for when? Who has plans for an entire evening?"

"Have you not told her about golems and their particularly lusty appetites?" Wembley gave Alex a chiding look.

"Sort of. But that's not the point. I have a window for time of death."

"Whoa—that's huge. Since when?" I asked.

"Since Star got entrepreneurial and extorted an additional thousand out of me via text."

"But...when..."

"While you were mooning over the detective. She wasn't certain she could do it, but after some experimentation—" He raised a hand. "Don't ask; I didn't. After some experimentation, she came up with a window for time of death."

"Which she then refused to reveal unless you contributed to the rugrats' college fund." I nodded. I didn't blame the woman. It was additional information he hadn't already paid for. And then again, four kids. "So?"

"Ten at night to one in the morning. Three hours is a little easier to pin down, and a lot of golems have an active social life in the evening."

Wembley nodded in agreement.

"Right. Can you send me the list? And I'll have Bradley do his magic...uh, that's not magic at all, but probably hacking. You know what I mean."

Alex was already tapping on his phone. My phone dinged with a message.

I pulled my phone out of my purse. "Got it." I forwarded it to Bradley with a quick and somewhat vague message about ten to one on the date of Dyson's death and any charges at that time. Then I included a note to call if he had questions.

Before I'd even put my phone away, I received a reply. I opened it and a broad grin spread across my face.

"What does the ever-industrious Bradley have to say for himself?" Alex asked.

"And I quote: 'What about cell calls with tower location?' He says he'll go ahead and look at that as well." I waggled my eyebrows. "Aren't you glad he's my sidekick?"

"I'm glad he's on our side," Alex said. "And let's hope that the app problem quietly disappears so he stays that way."

I closed my eyes on a groan. "And I'd just about forgotten. The prospect of Bradley's untimely and unjust murder is certainly enough to deflate my happy." I opened my eyes and scowled at him. "You really know how to burst a girl's bubble."

"It's not murder if it's an execution. And it looks like your designer is here." Alex stood up without looking an ounce repentant. "And I've got to get back to the office and review this information. Now that we have an approximate time of death—"

The doorbell interrupted him.

He tipped his head in the direction of the front door. "I told you. You really don't have vamp hearing, do you? Now that we have a time frame, I want to look at Gladys's timeline and Dyson's schedule. Maybe there's a clue hidden there."

"Call me if you come up with something?" When Alex nodded, I headed to the door and opened it. I greeted my designer with a polite smile, but it was forced. Alex was right. I really didn't want the house finished.

As Alex excused himself and slipped past my designer, I called after him, "Call me even if you don't find anything mind-blowing."

When I turned back to Bridgette, she was watching Alex depart with a keen eye.

"And you just married. Shame."

She winked. "A girl can look."

I closed the door behind her and said, "Maybe you can explain to me what it is that's so appealing about him. It's like he has this pheromone that attracts any woman in a twenty-foot radius."

"Really? You don't see it?"

As we walked into the kitchen, I tried to explain my confusion. "It's not that I can't tell he's handsome in that lean, tall, accountant-turned-bad boy way of his—"

"No, that's not it at all. He looks like a clean-cut, modern version of an old west sheriff."

I checked to make sure she wasn't kidding. Because that made no sense, and even if it did...no way. But she looked pretty sure. "Really? I don't see that at all. Huh."

"Enough about men, accountant or western hero, what are you thinking about the fixtures for the second bathroom? Did you look at the sample catalogue I left with you?"

Uh-oh. I totally had not. I looked around for Wembley, but he'd disappeared. I hollered toward the back of the house, "Wembley, I need you!"

Wembley would have the right answer. He always knew exactly what fixture and what tile and what flooring. I wish he'd agreed to make all these decisions for me. I sighed and waited for the house-flipping maestro to appear.

14

AN UNEXPECTED BOON

By the time Bridgette left, I realized I was starving. I headed into the kitchen for some carrot juice or maybe some spicy veggie juice—hm, maybe a mango-spinach smoothie.

I was considering my options when I almost ran into Wembley.

He stepped back and said, "Ah, a question."

"Can I eat and listen? Oh, and thanks for all the help with the fixtures and everything."

He waved away my thanks. "And yes, please eat. I can even make you a new version of that berry-veggie smoothie you tried the other day if you're interested."

I nodded eagerly. The original had been fantastic, so I had high expectations for the improved version.

"The lead that you and Alex had? I don't suppose that it came from one of his spirit contacts?"

I pinched my lips together. We'd sworn not to reveal each other's secrets. His: that he had well-established connections with a variety of entities, including spirits, elementals, and demons. And that sometimes those entities pestered him in an uncomfortable—possibly dangerous—way. Me: that I could see them—or had seen one of them once.

"You're sworn to secrecy?"

I shrugged with one shoulder but kept my lips sealed. I'd had a few issues with impulse control since my transformation. I occasionally felt like a kid trapped in an adult's body when it came to my ability to delay gratification, filter my speech, and act circumspectly. But I kept working on it, hoping it would get easier.

"Right. I'll assume you're sworn to secrecy. So let's assume the tip came from one of the spirits. I just want you to consider whether Alex's reluctance to rely on the information stems from the source."

I narrowed my eyes. I knew that Alex was not a fan of the wispy, ghostly creatures and thought they were treacherous. But he'd also said that they didn't outright lie. But then the tip had been a bit off. But—

"I'll just let you think about the fact that Alex brings all of his personal baggage to the table when he's dealing with those creatures. He doesn't think we're aware—but the people closest to him know. Maybe not everything, but we know he delved into the arcane when he was young and opened the doors wider to the spirit world than he should."

His connection with those creatures had to have something to do with the tattoos that covered his torso. Which raised the question: why not get them removed?

But magic was weird. Maybe they couldn't be removed using traditional methods. As I pondered Alex's connection with another plane, Wembley began yet another attempt to create a fully satisfying vegan meal. It was an uphill battle. Nothing seemed to be as filling as drinking blood. Not that I knew firsthand. I was going on my second month as a blood-free vamp, and that was just fine with me. But according to Wembley, it only took a few sips to satisfy, a little more to be full, and a pint was like a slice too many on pizza day. Not exactly his words, but the general idea.

"Voila." Wembley presented me with a frothy pinkish-purple concoction.

I sat down at the table and then took a sip. A sigh of pleasure slipped past my lips. "You added salt."

Wembley grinned. "I did: sea salt. Salt seems to be an important component for flavor, and I think what you crave flavor-wise might be indicative of the nutrients you need."

I sipped happily for a minute until I realized that Wembley was puttering around in the kitchen much longer than the little bit of cleanup he was doing required. "Was there something else?"

He glanced over his shoulder as if he hadn't a clue what I meant.

I set my half-full glass down. "You usually let me do the cleanup."

"Ah. It's about the house…" He abandoned what was becoming repetitive counter wiping to join me at the kitchen table. "You're taking longer than I'd planned with the remodel—"

"I'm sorry." I clasped my fingers around my cold drink and rubbed my thumb up and down the sweating surface, my eyes fixed on the mindless action. To fess up, or not to fess up? *Seem* pathetic and lonely, or *be* pathetic and lonely?

"No, it's not a problem. I just wondered if you'd changed your mind."

"About what?" Then I stopped fiddling with my glass and thought about what he'd said. "Oh! You think I have buyer's remorse. No. No way."

"You hate making decisions?" He quirked an eyebrow at

me. "You've been practically incapable of deciding on a single fixture or color without a lengthy discussion. Something's up."

I chugged the glass of berry-veggie smoothie, trying to give myself a little time to consider whether Alex might have been right about the whole roommate thing. Maybe Wembley wouldn't mind sharing the house longer term. I set the glass down with a wince. I scrunched up my face and waited for an unpleasant brain-freeze sensation to pass. Once I could speak again, I said, "Wanna be my roommate?"

Wembley grinned and leaned back in his chair. "I *am* your roommate."

"Not funny. Yes, no, or I'm a complete loon for asking. You have limited choices, so it should be easy to pick."

"Are you saying you enjoy my company? That you want me to live here after the work is done? That maybe you appreciate more than just my house-flipping skills?"

"Could you be any more obnoxious about this?" I asked. Obviously, he was cool with the idea. At least, it seemed so. "Is that a yes?"

"I get to keep the master?" When I nodded, he grinned. "Definitely a yes."

My phone rang, interrupting any possibility of rent negotiations or roommate contracts. I snatched it from the table and answered without looking at the display. I really didn't want to hash out details right now. "Hello?"

"I'm heading your way," Alex said.

"Did you find something in Gladys's schedule? Or Dyson's?" I glanced quickly at the screen to check that Bradley hadn't sent me an update, but I hadn't missed a text or received an email on my new Society-business-only account.

I put the phone back to my ear in time to hear, "No. Just checking you're home."

And he hung up.

I scowled at my phone. "That was Alex."

"And?"

"And nothing. Checking to see that I'm home and headed this way. The turkey hung up on me." I gave Wembley a sad look. "Any chance for a second shake before he shows up?"

"Absolutely." And Wembley hustled with that shake, because we both knew that something had blown up, and me running around hungry while trying to sleuth wasn't exactly ideal.

Wembley handed me the second shake a split second before a loud pounding on the door reverberated through the house.

"I'll let you get that. You're much better with Alex when he's in a mood." And Wembley retreated to the back of the house as I headed for the front door.

I wasn't entirely sure what he meant, because Alex was only a little moody, and I didn't know that I had any special talent for dealing with him when he was.

I mentally shrugged and opened the door.

To a massive red beast.

A slobbering, stinky red-furred monster.

I staggered back a step as two huge paws landed on my chest, and a long-eared, sad-looking hound dog stuck his muzzle in my face and inhaled my breath.

"Oh my God—what is he doing?" As I spoke, he sniffed almost delicately with his massive nose and then dropped to the ground into a sit.

Alex held a leash attached to a collar around the dog's

neck, but he dropped it and stepped inside and shut the door.

"Mallory, meet Boone. Boone, meet Mallory."

The dog's head tipped in Alex's direction when he said Boone.

"Why—"

"He needs a place to stay." Alex stopped, and I realized he was angry. Raging mad, in fact. A hint of a lavender gleam sparked in his eyes...or maybe I imagined it.

"What's happened?" I looked down at the dog, and then I remembered: I'd seen him before, coming out of Bits, Baubles, and Toadstools after he'd searched headquarters for traces of Dyson. "Where's..." But I couldn't remember his handler's name.

"Celia. His partner was Celia. She's dead."

A low, sighing whine escaped the dog, and he sank to the floor in a puddle of excess skin and ears.

I leaned down and rubbed the poor animal's ears. He leaned into my hand. "What happened?"

"A neighbor heard Boone howling in the yard and got concerned." Alex looked down at the dog. "When no one answered and she couldn't get in the house, she let herself into the yard to check on the dog and then called both the numbers on his tag. One is the emergency response number."

"I see."

Boone whimpered again, but didn't pick his head up. His loose lips puffed out with a tiny sigh, and my eyes started to burn.

"Good Lord, Mallory. Here." Alex squatted down next to the dog and handed me a hanky—a different one from this morning. This one was softer.

As I dabbed my eyes, I wondered if he had a stash in his car. So I asked.

"No, in my office. But with you getting teary over every little—"

"Hey, watch it." I gave Boone's ear a rub and a gentle tug then stood up. "It's been a stressful few weeks. Give a girl a break."

He stood up with me. "I wasn't criticizing, just saying demand has recently increased. Any chance you can keep him? Your place seemed like a good choice, what with you and Wembley both living here. And there's usually one of the two of you around. What?"

I realized I was bouncing up and down on my toes, so I rocked back on my heels. "Wembley said he'd stay."

Alex smiled, but he still looked ragged around the edges. And then the brief burst of excitement I'd felt over sharing my news lost its bloom. Because Celia. "You said she's dead. You're sure? She's not just missing?"

"No. She's definitely not missing."

Boone groaned and rolled over on his side.

"Can he understand us?" I whispered. Because if he could, he shouldn't hear whatever came next.

"I think so. He is a dog—but he's been connected with Celia for a long time." Alex tipped his head in the direction of the kitchen.

I nodded, then leaned down and said to Boone, "Stay... uh, please stay? If you don't mind."

His lips puffed out with another sigh, but he didn't lift his head.

"Good dog." I backed away slowly and watched him until I was halfway through the living room. I turned to find Alex watching me with a glimmer of amusement.

"You'll let him stay here?"

"Of course." I bit my lip. "What happened to her?"

His voice low, Alex said, "Anton found her in her bathroom, bound with bewitched rope and hung."

Poor Celia.

"You knew her?"

Alex took a deep breath. "And liked her. She was a good person. Anton brought the hound back to headquarters with Celia. With her body."

That poor dog... My eyes started to burn again. "It's no problem. He can definitely stay here."

"That's a relief. He seems to like you, and he wasn't particularly fond of Anton."

"Hmph. That's two of us." The big red dog went up a notch in my estimation. "Do you think Celia's murder is related to Dyson's?"

"Absolutely. Celia's been traveling for a while now. She's only recently back in town. She's hardly had a chance to run into troubles of her own. And she was involved with the investigation."

"About that." I indicated a chair at the table and sat down across from him. "What did she do that would have frightened the murderer? You said something about her and Boone checking for Dyson's scent—I don't get how that's a problem."

Alex closed his eyes, rolled his head back. "Yeah—that's not such a problem." When he opened his eyes, he looked pissed again. "Think about it. If we're right and Gladys is innocent and also the intended fall guy, Celia and Boone could have put a major kink in the frame-up."

I blinked. Then realized that if Boone and Celia could detect Dyson's scent at headquarters and even give an approximation of when he was last there... "The two of them could probably catalogue the people who'd been to

Gladys's house. Including the killer. Oh no. That's terrible. But wouldn't the killer—who's obviously a Society insider—have known what Boone and Celia could do?"

"I think a few pieces of the plan fell apart. If there were more than a few moving pieces, that could happen. Who could predict that Gladys would keep a cool head and bury the body?"

I nodded. Gladys didn't give the initial impression of one who acted with grace under fire. "Oh, and you said Celia and Boone had been out of town. Maybe the killer was surprised by her return."

"She cut her trip short. I don't know why. We haven't been close in some time. But I do know she came back early."

I checked the living room to see if Boone had gotten up—but also because I didn't want Alex to see the curiosity in my eyes. Because I definitely wondered exactly how close he and Celia had been.

"I think he'll be fine in the hallway," Alex said. "He's probably crashed out, after all the howling and the traveling in strange cars—and chasing Anton."

I swung my head back around. "I'm sorry—what?"

"Just checking to see if you were paying attention. But I don't think a murderer would plan for Boone and Celia. I think that was a complete oversight. Djinn aren't that common, and she's been in and out of town for a while with work. Also, she doesn't do much local work for the Society, so why would she be on the murderer's radar?"

"Gladys acts unpredictably, someone with the ability to identify the killer appears on the scene, and then there's the body. Surely the body was meant to be found. What do you think the killer is planning to do about that?"

"Maybe this was it. Kill Celia, thereby removing one

threat, and then wait to see the fallout?" Alex ran a hand through his already disheveled hair. "There are already awkward questions. Dyson's death can't go undiscovered indefinitely."

"Oh! An alibi—what if Gladys has an alibi for Celia's death? Is there a time of death?"

"Anton suspects that's when the dog pitched a fit. Remember the neighbor called? So there's a suspected time of death. The dog couldn't do anything because he was locked out of the house. Anton said the back door and the frame of the bedroom window were pretty torn up."

"Maybe Boone knows who did it—by scent or sight." The dog had looked upset—because his partner was dead or because he'd been traumatized by experiencing her death? "Oh no; no, this could be bad. If that's true, he could be in danger, couldn't he?" The thought made the hair prickle on the back of my neck.

"I don't think so, or I wouldn't have brought him here. I also don't think he'll be much help. Celia had a mind-to-mind link with him. Some djinn have that ability. But without it, I'm not sure that we can get any information from him."

"Boone?" I called out.

The click of nails preceded him into the kitchen. He wasn't moving very fast.

"Did you guys check him out for injuries?" As soon as I said injury, Boone sat in front of me and lifted up his right foot. "The nails look pretty chewed up. Aw. This one is bleeding." I shot Alex a disappointed look.

"Don't even start. He's obviously walking around and not limping. We had other concerns, remember?"

I wrinkled my nose. "Sorry."

Boone rested his head in my lap. There really wasn't that

much drool now that he'd cooled off from the car ride. I lifted up his lip to find his gums scraped and bits of wood embedded. "Oh, this isn't good. Let me get my tweezers."

I wasn't sure if I was talking to Alex or Boone. Weird to imagine a dog understanding my words.

Boone cocked his head and then backed up, giving me room to get up.

When I came back, tweezers in hand, Alex was quizzing Boone.

"Did you see the person who hurt Celia?" Alex asked.

No response from Boone, who had sprawled on the floor once again.

"Did you smell the person who hurt Celia? Do you have any idea what I'm asking you?"

As I got closer, Boone perked up. I sat back in my chair, and he got up to sit in between my legs and rested his muzzle on my leg.

I looked down at the droopy dog and said, "I think he understands me. But I don't think he gets you, Alex." I lifted up the dog's lip and started to remove little splinters in his gum line.

"I had to try." Alex rubbed his eyes. "If we don't get a break soon, we're going to have to tell Cornelius about having Dyson's body on ice."

I groaned. "I get it—but poor Gladys." I turned back to Boone and started on the other side of his mouth. "I wish you had some idea of who hurt your partner."

Boone's long, droopy ears perked up, and he lifted his head off my leg.

"Did you see that?" I asked.

"Yeah. Ask him a question."

I turned to look at Alex and gave him an exasperated look. "And how exactly is he supposed to respond?"

"Good grief, Mallory, just try it."

I blew out an annoyed breath—one that sounded a little like a growl. Then I looked at Boone's sad face, and asked, "Do you know who killed Celia?"

A funny noise made the hair on my neck stand at attention. Then it got louder and I realized the dog was growling. Another second and the sound was unmistakable. His lip lifted on one side of his muzzle to reveal a wicked-looking canine.

"There's your answer," Alex said.

I shot Alex an annoyed look. "Boone. I'm sorry, buddy."

The noise stopped suddenly.

"So what do I do, bring Boone with us wherever we go and hope that he points out the killer?"

A loud thud startled me.

"Yes." Alex pointed to the dog's wagging tail, thudding against the kitchen wall.

"That's not suspicious at all, toting a hundred pound dog around with me everywhere." I shook my head. "I'm still practicing regularly with Tangwystl, but I'm not actually much good at defending myself. I don't really want to be a walking target if we can avoid it."

"He has anxiety."

I grinned. "Sold." I looked at Boone. "I know you're a brave dog, and you're on your best behavior, but we're going to fib to a bunch of people and tell them I can't leave you at home because you're so distraught you're eating my house. Sound good?"

"Wawoooo." Boone's tail thudded against the kitchen wall again.

"Well, I guess that's agreement." Alex glanced at his cell phone. "I need to get back to headquarters. Anton is finishing up at Celia's. We're hoping for some indication of the killer, but I'm not holding my breath. He's also going to gather up Boone's supplies. Once I let him know you've agreed to dog-sit, he'll drop everything off here."

I'd thought Alex was dropping off Boone in a more permanent capacity, so when he said dog-sit it tugged a little at my heart. Which was silly. I didn't even know Boone.

A cold nose touched my fingers, and I looked down to find his red head near my fingertips. I ran my hand along the soft fur of his head and down one of his long ears. "Think I have time to head over to Gladys's for a face-to-face chat about her alibi?"

Alex glanced up from his phone. "I'll let Anton know to leave everything on the porch if no one's home." He tapped on his phone, and when he was done updating Anton, I'd already found Boone's discarded leash and attached it to his collar.

"Let's go, Boone-dog." I grabbed my purse on the way to the door, and hollered over my shoulder, "Home soon, Wembley!"

Alex opened the door for Boone and I, and said, "You guys need a message board or something."

That sounded like an excellent idea, especially since Wembley was now my real roomie. Such a small thing, but it made me happy.

I approached the passenger side of the Grand Cherokee, but Boone walked to the back, pulling me with him. Up until that point, he'd been an absolute gentleman.

"I think he likes to ride in the back," Alex said. He opened the back door and started to fold the seats down.

And that was when it occurred to me: "Boone would never have fit in my sports car."

"You say that like it's some surprising statement. But no, I don't think Boone would have fit very well in your tiny and very sporty Audi." He popped his head out from the other side of the car, where he was finishing with the seats. "We're not talking about precognition again, are we? I don't know why Wembley keeps filling your head with that garbage."

"Well, I had a strong urge to buy this particular car, and here I am a few weeks later taking care of a giant dog." I popped the back hatch. "That's pretty darn handy, wouldn't you say?"

Boone hopped into the back and immediately laid down. He wasn't quite smiling, but he looked a little less sad than he had before. I closed the hatch with a solid thud, and Boone didn't blink.

"Start the car and get the air conditioning working before you fry your dog." Alex stepped to the driver's door and opened it. Once I'd climbed in and closed the door, he motioned for me to roll the window down and said, "Be careful. Please."

"Pshaw. I'm going to Gladys's house. What are you worried about?" And I backed out of my drive without waiting for Alex to respond.

15

BOONE TELLS ALL...ALMOST

As I pulled into Gladys's driveway, I got both a text and a phone call at almost the same time. I ignored the text and answered the call. "Hello?"

"Hi, this is Rachael Dyson. Mallory?"

"Yes, hi, Rachael."

"Do you have a minute to speak with me? I understand that you're investigating my father's disappearance."

"Of course. I'd be happy to speak with you. Would you like to set up a meeting? Alex and I can come out as soon as you're available."

There was a brief pause on the line and then Rachael said, "No. I don't think a meeting is necessary. And with Alex, it's awkward, because..."

I rolled my eyes. The man was a dating menace. "No, no —I'm glad to speak with you on the phone. I'm sorry we missed you earlier today. Let me just get a pen." I started to dig around in my purse, but Rachael interrupted me.

"Well, I don't have much to say, just that I didn't want you looking in the wrong place. Mother thinks she knows what Dad is up to all day long, but she really doesn't have a clue. I mean, she knows where the money is, but not how Dad spends his time."

"You think your father is participating in some kind of risky behavior that might have led to his disappearance?" I pulled a pen out of my purse with a flourish. Whatever Rachael said, I was taking notes. Now, paper...

"He sleeps around, but that's not so odd, and I can't imagine anyone wanting to kidnap him over such a thing. He's careful to only get involved with single women."

"Your dad has a type?"

"Oh yes. His girlfriends all look just like Mother. Tall and red-headed are prerequisites; the rest seems to be negotiable." Rachael sounded amused and not at all dismayed by her father's behavior.

I tore out a deposit slip from my checkbook and made a few notes on the back. Rachael. Lots of girlfriends, red hair, tall. "So if not women, what were you thinking?"

Rachael paused. She'd called with some purpose in mind, but she was having difficulty spitting out whatever it was she wanted me to know. I waited—not so patiently, but I waited.

"Dad doesn't actually run his own companies anymore." She spoke quickly, all the words coming out in a rush.

"If your dad isn't running his companies, who is?"

"Oh, Becky, of course."

I scribbled: Becky running Dyson's business. Time to call Becky again. But then my mind leapt to embezzlement. And if Dyson noticed, that might be why he was dead. "So, you think we're looking in the wrong place?"

"I don't know. I just didn't want you making decisions purely based on Mother's flawed information. Dad spends most of his daytime hours reading and keeping abreast of world news and his nighttime hours chasing women. And he has for years."

"Red-headed women."

Rachael laughed, but it was a strained, sad sound. "I have no idea where that obsession originated—not with Mother—but yes."

"Is there anything else you can think of that might help our investigation?" I didn't have the heart to ask her where she thought her father might have gone. I just couldn't do it.

"No. I just can't believe this happened. I mean, just a few more years and he'd have officially retired. I think he dreaded the change in his social status, though." She groaned. "And Mother would never have let him live it down. She loved being the wife of the Society's CEO."

And now Rachael sounded like she knew her father wasn't coming back. My eyes started to burn and I yanked a hanky out of my purse, one of Alex's. I'd meant to return it to him after it had been laundered.

I dabbed at my eyes, and said, "Thank you for reaching out, Rachael. If you think of anything else that might be important, don't hesitate to call me."

After Rachael hung up, I sat in the car with the air conditioning blowing in my face. I was happier as a vamp—truly I was. But since my human self had died, I'd been bombarded with death. I flipped the vanity mirror open and checked my eyes. Pink, but not horribly so.

There was more death in my life now. And more crime. More deceit. I looked over my shoulder at Boone. "You know, for someone who's not quite technically alive in the normal, aging-grow-old-and-die way, and who does a lot of illegal and dangerous stuff, I really am pretty happy."

Boone looked back with his big brown eyes, framed by his droopy ears and all that red fur.

"And I think you're a lot happier than you look most of the time, although I know you're having a rough time right now."

His ears perked up and his tail thudded on the floor of the car once. Twice. Three times.

"I'll take that as agreement, Boone-dog. Wanna go inside?"

Boone stood up and looked out the back window expectantly.

When I went around the back to let him out, I realized I didn't have any of his special stuff. He'd been wearing a bright orange and black harness when I saw him and Celia at headquarters, and his leash had been a lot longer than the one I had. Oh well. We'd work with what we had.

I popped the hatch open and quickly grabbed his leash. "Wouldn't want you to run out in the street and get hit by a car or anything."

He tipped his head, making one ear hang down much lower than the other, then his big brown eyes darted to the quiet residential street and back to me. He waited patiently for me to move out of the way and then jumped down from the back.

"Right. I got it. But what if there was a bunny or a squirrel?"

Boone smiled. I'd bet that was what he was doing. The corners of his mouth turned up, just like on a person. The dog was laughing at me, I was sure.

The hatch closed with a solid thump. And after reeling in his leash, Boone and I headed for the front door.

Except we didn't get far.

Boone's head dropped to the ground, and he took off down the driveway toward the street. Then he stopped, lifted his head, and did a U-turn toward the house. His head dropped down again and he followed his nose up the driveway, paused to smell the flowerbeds next to the walkway, and after a few deep breaths zoomed ahead. Suddenly, I was standing in front of the front door, and Boone had his nose glued to the seam of the door.

I was about to knock when he jumped up, put two paws on Gladys's very clean, white-painted door, and then dropped down to the ground and rocked back on his haunches in a sit. A very alert sit.

I knocked, but I couldn't quite take my eyes off Boone. He was staring at the door with a disturbing intensity. Then his lip lifted and a quiet growl reached my ears.

"You've got it, don't you?" I leaned down closer, the sound growing as I closed the gap between us. I whispered, "You have the killer's scent, don't you?"

The growl got louder. I could feel it reverberating in my gut. I'd say that was a resounding yes.

I stood up, uncertain what to do now, since Gladys didn't appear to be home. "That'll teach me not to call ahead." I turned away, but Boone didn't come with me. "Hey, buddy, we may have to come back later. I get that you found a clue, but I don't think she's in."

Boone didn't turn when I spoke. He jumped up on the door again, but this time he scrambled at it with his claws.

"Oh, Boone! Don't do that, please." And then the metaphorical light bulb came on. Boone's claws were ragged from scratching at the door and window frame of the house while—so we'd assumed—the killer had his or her terrible way with Celia.

"Oh, no. No, no, no." I dropped Boone's leash and grabbed at the doorknob. Locked. Brain in a jumble, I tried to think if there was a way in.

The back door...in the backyard. Or the side door into

the garage. Side door first, I thought as I made a dash for the side of the house.

"Make some noise!" I called over my shoulder at the hound still pawing, now frantically, at the door.

"Wawooo. Wawoo." The sound of Boone's combination bark-bay faded as I turned the corner of the house.

I just hoped the neighbors would take note and call— "Good grief." They'd call the police. I went through the back gate, looked for the side door... There. But when I tried it, the handle wouldn't turn.

I jumped over some flowerbeds and headed to the back door—and then I heard the garage door opening. And Boone was still at the front of the house.

Reversing my path, I hopped the flowerbeds and ran through the gate, visions of an injured Boone flashing through my mind. I hadn't a clue if he understood the concept of traffic, so what had I been thinking to drop his leash?

As I rounded the corner, I got a nice side profile of Gladys driving away in her Volvo wagon.

"What the heck?" I stood in the driveway, watching her speed away, when Boone bumped my dangling hand with his head.

When I looked down at him, his eyes were boring a hole through that retreating car, and he growled. Once the wagon disappeared down a side street, he ran back to the front door and scratched.

"Okay, I really don't get it. I'm sorry."

I watched him in dismay as he loped around to the side gate I'd left open in my earlier, hurried sprint. A high-pitched, yipping bark emerged from the backyard.

"Wait a second!" Now I had visions of him launching himself through a glass window.

Unlike at his partner Celia's house, there were massive picture windows in the backyard. I ran like the devil was on my tail.

When I got to the back door, Boone gave one final yip and backed away from the door. I tried the door and the knob turned under my fingers. As I stepped through the door, I considered maybe I wasn't doing the smartest thing —and for the first time, I realized, I should have called Alex.

I stopped and pointed a finger at Boone. "Stay." And then pulled my phone out and headed inside. I kept my eyes on the room, but when it looked like no one was there, lurking, waiting to attack swordless me, I called Alex.

He picked up immediately. "Everything okay?"

"Nope. Head this way, right now." I tapped speaker and put the phone in my pocket. "I'm inside Gladys's house and something is up. She wouldn't answer her door and drove off like a crazy person down the road." To the right was the kitchen and the left the bedrooms. I headed left.

"What are you doing right now?"

My peripheral vision caught movement, and I spun around to find Boone shadowing me. "I told you to stay."

"Are you talking to me? And are you inside the house?" Alex sounded more than a little put out. And I could hear the sound of a car door slamming in the background. At least he was on the way, annoyed or not.

"Not talking to you, and definitely inside the house." I glanced down at Boone. "I'm not alone; Boone is with me."

The dog let out a small sigh.

I put my finger to my lips, but he just blinked innocently.

"Leave. Now."

"No." I headed down the hallway where all of the bedrooms were located.

"Please tell me Tangwystl is with you."

"Uh..."

Before I could answer, Boone bolted down the hallway, his leash trailing behind.

"Gotta run—just a second."

That dog was fast. I caught up to him in the bedroom, sitting next to a prone woman.

"Alex, I just found someone."

I could hear indistinct cursing in the background. "Who is it?"

She was lying on the floor, curled on her side with her back to me, and her red hair fell across her face obscuring her features. But that red hair was awfully familiar.

I leaned down and pushed the hair back, hoping that I was wrong—or that I was right and she wasn't dead—but mostly that nothing terrible would be under that mass of fiery red hair.

"Gladys," I whispered after I'd tucked the last stray strands away from her face.

"What? I can't hear you. Did you say Gladys?" Alex grumbled when I didn't immediately answer, but I was too busy trying to figure out if she was still alive.

Did vampires have a pulse? I had one—so I was going with yes. Kneeling next to her, I couldn't see if she was breathing—but for all I knew, that was normal. I felt at her wrist for a pulse, but couldn't find one.

As I poked and pushed at her neck with two fingers, hunting for some sign of life, her eyelashes fluttered and her eyes opened. Only a flicker of confusion showed on her face, then it was gone and her clear eyes stared into mine. "Can you untie me?"

"Uh, sure." I hadn't noticed that she'd been tied, but then I realized she meant her feet.

"I could do it myself, but I'm feeling a little weak." And then she was gone again, just like that.

"Gladys!" I tapped her cheek lightly several times, but there was no response. "Alex?"

I pulled my phone out of my pocket, but I must have hung up on him at some point.

I blew out a breath. "Boone, she better not be dead."

But Boone didn't have anything to say this time.

Since I didn't know vamp CPR—or even if vamps *needed* CPR—I decided to untie her first. That way, if she came around, she'd at least be more comfortable. I'd gotten one of the knots out and was working on the second when it occurred to me I didn't know with certainty that this woman *was* Gladys. Maybe the woman in the Volvo had been the real Gladys.

I sat cross-legged at the maybe-not-real Gladys's feet and considered my options. "Not the real Gladys or the real Gladys?" If she was the real one, the killer had surely been zooming away in Gladys's car. If mine was the fake, then the real Gladys had been fleeing for her life and in her panic may not have even seen me.

"Are you meditating?"

"Ack!" My entire body flinched.

Alex stood in the doorway, looking like he hadn't just busted every speed limit between here and headquarters.

16

DEAD VAMPS DON'T BREATHE

"What are you doing?" he asked.

I stood up. "Trying to decide if Gladys is dead or not." I looked at the still form on the ground. "And if that's actually Gladys."

Alex walked in the room, and in about ten seconds had untied the woman, picked her up, and placed her gently on the bed—making me feel a little foolish and very useless in the process.

"Why would you think that's not Gladys?"

But I had more pressing concerns. "She's not dead, right?"

He closed his eyes and shook his head. When he opened them, he said, "Not dead. You need to have a chat with Wembley about what normal looks like for every other vampire but you. They don't have a very strong pulse, but there is one. And she's warm. And breathing."

I gave him a sheepish look. "I couldn't see her chest move." Then I shrugged. "Wait, why isn't she awake? If she's still alive... Oh, and you're sure she's Gladys? Because I saw

Gladys—or a Gladys lookalike—driving away in Gladys's car."

Alex gave me an exasperated look as he pulled out his cell phone. "That would have been a good place to start." He tapped his phone then said, "Or at least after you took off the bewitched rope. That's what knocked her out. Sustained contact— Hey, Anton? Can you find Gladys Winston's silver Volvo Cross Country? I don't have the plates. It's possible the woman driving the car is Celia's killer. Yes, she's here. Yes, she is too. No, this is not somehow all Mallory's fault." He looked directly at me as he said the last part, then ended the call and pocketed his phone.

What was Anton's issue with me? He might look like Mr. Clean, but a really unpleasant, mean version. Everyone knew Mr. Clean was an amiable kinda guy. I had to swallow a chuckle, because it occurred to me there might actually be a real Mr. Clean running around in the world. Why not? Vamps, wizards, and witches were alive and kicking. What was one big bald animated guy that liked to keep house in comparison to a horde of bloodsucking vampires?

Focus, Mallory.

"The rope?" I asked. "You were saying about the rope?"

"Bewitched. And hard to come by. The longer it stays in contact with someone's skin, the deeper the sleep. Until the magic wears off or is used up, anyway."

I winced. "Oh. Well, I didn't know that, and I wasn't sure she was Gladys."

"Because the real Gladys would have access to bewitched rope and manage to tie up the killer so that she could escape?" Alex scratched his chin. "Actually, knowing Gladys, that second part isn't completely impossible."

"Right? And I didn't know about the magical rope. Is

there some indication of magical properties that I should be aware of?"

Alex picked up the discarded rope from the ground and handed it to me.

I took it reluctantly, because I didn't particularly want to pass out.

"It has to form a loop for the sedative effect to be triggered." Alex walked over to Boone and stroked his head. "Good dog." In a much lower voice, he said, "At least you kept her alive."

"Hey," I said as I fingered the rope. "I kept me alive."

Boone leaned against Alex's leg and looked generally self-satisfied. Traitorous dog.

And then, when I wasn't really paying attention, I caught it: a tiny hum of vibration. I chucked the rope at Alex. "I was supposed to feel that minuscule bit of magic how, exactly? And when?" Although I had actually untied one of the knots...

"Now you know to look and what to look for. Ah, sleeping beauty might be coming to."

Gladys's eyelashes fluttered, just like before, and then she opened her eyes. She took a breath and sat up. "Where is she?"

I'd bet Gladys was a morning person. She seemed to have a lot of practice waking up and being immediately clear-headed. Yet another intriguing and unexpected quality. Gladys was full of surprises.

"Maybe you'd like to answer that, Mallory," Alex said. "Mallory and Boone just saved you from a premature end."

Gladys nodded. "She was going to kill me."

"Wait, the Gladys lookalike spoke with you?" I couldn't even begin to envision how that conversation went down.

Gladys stood up, and Alex moved forward to steady her. Once she'd stopped teetering, she said, "Of course she didn't speak with me. I knew she was going to kill me because she showed up looking like me and attacked me. What else could her plan have been?"

Naturally...

"I don't suppose there's an evil twin lurking around—from your pre-vamp past, maybe?" I asked.

Both Gladys and Alex looked at me like I was a little kid sitting at the grownups table.

"Give me a break," I said. "Do you guys have another way to explain how Gladys attacked herself?"

"Glamor," Alex said.

And at the same time, Gladys said, "Illusion." And she was a newbie vamp, too, so that made me feel especially ignorant.

"Ah. So, any chance we know who can build that strong of a glamor?" I wasn't sure I knew anything about illusion magic. Persuasion was one thing; it involved changing the way one felt about something that was actually there. Alex had explained that. Illusion, though, meant changing what was observed.

"No, but I certainly know someone on the list who has some illusion skill."

"Right, the coyote, Becky." I thought my brain was going to explode. "But I thought she adored Dyson? And not only that—if it's Becky, it can't be Ophelia." I frowned at Alex. "I'd really like it to be Ophelia; she's so..." I could feel my nose wrinkling up. "She's so unrepentantly guilty. Whether she did it or not, she's guilty of something."

"Will you get over Ophelia already? Golems are different culturally from some of the other enhanced humans." Alex paused, and I could see the wheels turning. If he made a born versus made argument, I would thwack him. He said, "What you see as guilt is just a set of cultural norms: blunt, sexually adventurous, typically in open marriages."

Gladys nodded with a knowing air. "They like sex a lot, as a general rule. Blaine told me so."

"Who's Blaine?" I asked.

Alex looked away and started to fiddle with his keys.

Uh-oh. This should be good.

"He's a vampire. You should have seen him at the orientation. The one I haven't qualified to attend yet. He was there, and I'm sure very hard to miss." There was a flirtatious tone to her voice I'd certainly never heard before.

"Are you dating this guy?" I asked. You'd think with all the progress we'd been making with her reactions to men, she'd have let me in on such a big achievement.

She tipped her head. "Dating? No." She grinned. "Sex, yes. I didn't think you'd approve."

I blinked. No clue where she got that idea, but she'd made more progress than anticipated. "He's still around... somewhere, right?"

I could have smacked myself. Of course the guy was still around. Having hypothesized that Gladys might snap in an intimate moment did not mean that she actually would.

"Not here. He wouldn't have let someone else tie me up —I'm pretty sure about that." The look Gladys gave me indicated she wasn't sure if I was all there.

And Alex didn't look at me at all. He ducked his head and started tapping away on his phone.

I just shook my head and did a quick rejiggering in my head of exactly how far Gladys had come since her meltdown at headquarters a few weeks ago. Very far. She'd come very far. Divorced Diva parties, some (maybe a lot of) vamp-cultural acclimation, yoga-and meditation-induced stress relief, and time. It looked like Gladys was well on her way to a well-adjusted future life as a vamp. Assuming she'd keep living.

And I'd completely forgotten to ask about her alibi. "Gladys, any chance you remember what you were doing midday today?"

"What does that have to do with Blaine?" When I shook my head, she frowned and said, "Shopping with Louisa and Darla. Darla drove. We met at her house about ten, but maybe ten thirty."

Alex stopped fiddling with his phone and said, "When did you get home?"

"Late afternoon. We had lunch and drinks, then Louisa had a meltdown." She shrugged. "So we had some more drinks."

Alex nodded and resumed typing on his phone.

"Wait." I pointed a finger at Alex. "Are we coming in from the cold?"

Alex quirked an eyebrow. "If you mean, are we releasing all of the relevant details to the chief security officer of the Society—yes."

I gave him a disapproving look.

He returned it with a bland, what-else look.

I'd come to Gladys's to determine if she had an alibi and could be cleared. Well, that and to have Boone eliminate her once and for all as a suspect. So I guessed I couldn't blame Alex for spilling the beans to Cornelius. "Okay. Fine."

He bent his head down and started tapping again. "Done," he said, then pocketed his phone. He pointed to Gladys. "We're dropping you at headquarters."

"I assume we're headed to Becky's place?" I tried not to bounce on my toes—but how exciting that we'd managed to root out the evildoer and were so close to catching her. "Wait, how sure are we that it's Becky?" Because I was starting to realize we had no real proof against her, either. Though there certainly was ample opportunity for her to plan and execute Dyson's murder, as intimately familiar as she was with every aspect of his life.

"We're *not* sure. We're looking for evidence. Remember, that little thing called proof?" Alex indicated the door.

Boone, who was apparently worn out by all of the sniffing and running around, had planted himself across the doorway—but he got up at that point.

I swallowed a grumble and marched through the bedroom doorway, snagging Boone's leash on the way. Of course I remembered evidence was required. We wouldn't actually *turn in* anyone without proof. Maybe accuse... "I'm allowed to speculate freely during our investigation."

"Ah-huh."

Once in the hallway, Alex and I waited for Gladys to retrieve her purse. When she came back, she said, "You two are funny. You're like a married couple." She breezed past us and opened the front door. As she walked out onto the porch, she said over her shoulder, "But not the kind about to get a divorce."

I had to wonder how many couples Gladys knew that weren't divorced, divorcing, or headed that way. I very particularly did not look at Alex to see his response.

Alex had parked in the street but I'd pulled into the driveway, and it occurred to me that I could have stopped the killer in her—or his—tracks. If only... "I should have parked on the other side of the driveway."

"No, that wouldn't have helped." When we both turned to look at Gladys, she pushed a heavy curl behind her ear and said, "I would have just tapped the bumper and backed your car down the driveway, if I were the killer." Then she smiled. "In a way, it kind of was me, wasn't it? Oh!" She snapped her fingers. "The woman was wearing a wig."

Boone looked up at the snap, and Alex stopped in his tracks. I assumed I would follow him with Boone in the Jeep, but he did a U-turn and walked back to my car. "I'll just put one of these seats up."

It took just a second and Gladys had a seat in the back.

Once they were all loaded, Boone in the far back, Alex driving, and me in the front passenger seat, Alex said, "Gladys, tell me about this wig."

It took several minutes to get the details from Gladys, but, apparently, the person who'd attacked her had been in disguise.

"And that made the illusion easier to maintain, especially when added with the ability to alter how you feel about the person." Alex pulled onto the freeway, driving a little faster than usual. Nowhere near chase speed, but we weren't dawdling.

I checked to make sure that Alex could easily split attention without squishing us on a piling—then remembered he had fantastic reflexes. "Yeah, I don't get it. I mean, I get why the killer would want to disguise themselves. Minimize witnesses and all." I looked out the window at the suburban neighbor we were traveling through. "Gladys comes and goes throughout the day, and I'm sure no one's keeping track of when, so a neighbor could see the killer arrive and think nothing of it, assuming the killer was Gladys. But with illusion skills, why would the killer use a physical disguise?"

Gladys was busy petting Boone and didn't seem to be paying much attention, but you never knew with Gladys.

"Imagine you've had a glass of wine, a large meal, and you're with people you like. You might be likelier to trust what someone says if you're in a receptive frame of mind. That's persuasion." Alex glanced at me, and when I nodded, he said, "Now imagine you have some level of illusion skill, but you can't make a person see something that simply isn't there."

"Ah. Make yourself look as similar as possible through mundane means, give a little mental persuasion push, and then add a veneer of superficial illusion—got it. Sounds very coyote to me. At least, it fits within your description of a coyote's skills."

Alex nodded.

I considered our suspect list. "It's a woman; it has to be. Let's recap. We've got a handful of golem women in the community. Oh, yeah, I got a text ages ago. I bet it was Bradley." I pulled out my phone, and sure enough, the text I'd missed earlier was from him. "He just says all clear except Wendi. Any idea who Wendi is?"

"Ah, she shouldn't have been on the list. She's not out in public yet. Another peculiarity to golems. They're created as adults and spend their first several years of maturation secluded from the main stream of society."

So weird, but I'd bet they thought the concept of messy, spitting-up, diaper-wearing infants was pretty weird.

"Okay, so the female golem population is excluded. Wait —did we have Rachael and Ophelia on that list?"

"*We* did not. It was specifically a list of the other female golems on the Society's rolls."

I tapped a quick message to Bradley, but then I saw there were two texts from him, and I'd missed the first one. "Oops, hang on a sec; I missed part of the text." I scrolled down, and after I'd read the brief message I summarized it for Alex. "Nothing on Rachael—credit card or cell—and Ophelia was home. Does that mean Rachael turned off her cell phone?"

"It means Rachael doesn't have an alibi—and Ophelia and the other women have partially confirmed alibis."

I wrinkled up my nose. He was annoyingly right. The location of a cell phone did not equal the location of a person. I called Bradley.

He answered on the first ring. "Hello, Mallory."

"Hey, Bradley. Thanks for the information. Was there anyone else on that list who was at home like Ophelia?"

"No." No hesitation, so either Bradley had the list in front of him or an exceptional memory.

"Anything noteworthy about the locations?" I asked.

"All but one was in the downtown area and several had credit card transactions for large quantities of alcohol."

I grinned. "Let me guess: around Sixth Street?"

"In that area, yes. The one outlier was in Dallas with corresponding Dallas-area purchases to suggest a trip: gas, restaurant meals, hotel charges."

"Got it. That's useful info. Thanks."

I was about to end the call when Bradley said, "Do you want the financial information?"

"Sorry?"

"You asked for background information, and I have some financial details that might be important. I just put them together and was going to send you an email."

"Yes—that would be great if you found something noteworthy." I covered the phone with my hand and said to Alex, "He's got some financial stuff."

Alex didn't look too interested, so I didn't put it on speaker.

"The Dyson elders' holdings have decreased by twenty percent in the last five years," Bradley said.

"Dyson elders? You mean Reginald and Ophelia?" When Bradley confirmed, I asked, "Does Rachael have a lot of property in her name?"

"Yes. Her holdings have been increasing in value over the last fifty years."

"Did you say fifty years?" That couldn't be right. Ophelia looked maybe old enough to have a teenage daughter, but... Golems. Right.

"Yes, that's correct. There was some obfuscation through the creation of different business entities, but the information is there." Bradley paused. "It did take me some time to sort out the specific details, hence the delay."

"Twenty-four hours isn't a delay, Bradley. You're a star. Thank you."

"You're welcome," he said, and hung up.

I checked the back seat to find Gladys paying us no attention at all and lavishing Boone with attention. Since the hound had saved her life, he certainly deserved it.

"What was that all about?" Alex asked.

I tried to remember what exactly Ophelia had told him about the family finances. Something about them being solid? "The Dysons' finances. Did you know that Reginald and Ophelia's holdings have taken a twenty percent nose dive recently?"

His eyebrows climbed. "No. In fact, Ophelia gave the distinct impression that there had been no recent changes."

"Well, maybe recent is relative. Bradley says the last five years."

"In the land of enhanced humans, that's very recent." Alex chewed over that bit of news for a few seconds then said, "And Rachael?"

"Quite flush. You think she's embezzling?"

Alex passed a car with a little too much enthusiasm, and I swayed in my seat.

"No," he said. "No...I don't think so." He didn't sound nearly as certain of her innocence as he had previously.

"If she's flush—embezzlement or no—then she has no immediate need of her half of the family's remaining wealth."

Alex looked uncomfortable—because of his previous relationship with Rachael? He really got around, and that had to create difficulties, as small and long-lived as the enhanced community was. Well, he'd have to suck it up...or stop sleeping with everyone in the community.

I shook my head—enough with the speculation over Alex's love life. "Ophelia, the less-than-loving wife who actually admits to wanting her husband dead, still looks like a fabulous suspect to me. She also tried to bribe us to provide proof—and I think finish him off."

The switch in focus away from Rachael seemed to ease some of his tension. "Which makes no sense if she's the killer, because she would know that he was already dead."

Not party-mad golem women boozing it up on Sixth Street, not Ophelia, not Rachael—or, at least, Alex was hoping not, from what I could tell—who was left?

"It has to be Becky, then," I said.

"We'll see. I'd prefer a little more concrete evidence before we turn her over to the Society. A voluntary confession would be ideal, but another bewitched rope in her possession or even a red wig at this point would be some evidence of her guilt."

I huffed in annoyance—*I* wasn't the inquisition in this equation—and glanced over my shoulder, looking for some support from Gladys. But Gladys was conked out. Her head was tipped to the left, resting against her shoulder and the headrest. "Are we sure that Gladys is going to be okay?"

Alex looked in the rearview mirror then grinned. "Don't worry; she's still alive."

"Okay..." I glanced back at her again, but I couldn't see how he could tell. "How difficult would it be to get that bewitched rope?"

"Very. And that's why it's one of the first pieces of solid evidence that we've had. Not just one, but two bewitched pieces of rope. One was used in Celia's death, and now this one. And in both instances, the killer was interrupted. That has to be why she left them at the scene, because she had to know they'd implicate her."

I had a guilty twinge. "We left the rope at Gladys's."

"It's in my pocket."

"Oh."

Alex's lips twitched. "You'll figure it out."

I squirmed uncomfortably in my seat. I *was* awfully new at sleuthing. And vamping, come to think of it. "Hey, who's this Blaine guy?"

All signs of amusement vanished from Alex's face, and when he answered, his tone was neutral. Carefully neutral. "Blaine Waldrup. He's a developer, so it's no surprise that Austin is an appealing location. I believe he'd outstayed his welcome in Tampa." Alex caught my curious look and said, "He lived too long in one place without aging."

"Ah." So many new problems that I couldn't keep up with all the vampy issues I'd be facing. But at least having to tackle that one was a little way off.

"You didn't notice him at orientation?" Alex asked, again with a neutral tone.

"No. Why? Should I have?"

Alex shrugged.

I checked on Gladys and saw that her head had sunk further to the left. Her left hand rested on Boone. Surely he'd look less relaxed if she'd just died in the back seat? I squinted and stared at her chest.

And then I caught it: the neckline of her dress shifted slightly. "Ha! Gotcha." I almost did a fist pump, but stopped and blushed when I saw that Alex was peering at my curiously. Staring at a woman's cleavage to determine whether she'd croaked in the back of my car was super odd—I could hardly avoid that conclusion.

"You know, vampires don't blush." Alex said it with a smile in his voice, so I wasn't sure if he was teasing me for a completely normal vamp reaction or just amused by my weirdness.

So I ignored him. I wasn't about to explain that I was throwing a party for myself because I'd seen Gladys take a breath.

"She's still alive. It's just the residual effect of the rope."

I pinched my lips together. The man was practically telepathic. But his mention of the rope reminded me that it was a key piece of evidence—and a rare piece of bewitched equipment. "The Society's CEO would have had access to the rope, right?"

He nodded. "Cornelius's staff are responsible for maintaining a magical arsenal, but Dyson has ultimate control of... What? What's wrong?"

I hadn't even realized I'd winced. I tried to look less guilty, and said, "Ah, about that. Becky has been running the show from behind the scenes. I completely forgot—I got a call earlier from Rachael. Apparently, Dyson's interest in anything but retirement has been on the decline for a while. It's actually Becky who runs his day-to-day business and Society affairs."

I figured there was no point in mentioning that Dyson's semi-retirement had basically meant screwing as many red-headed women as possible while simultaneously avoiding his responsibilities and making his assistant do all the work. The man was dead, after all.

"That might have been useful to know," Alex said.

As if I didn't feel guilty enough about forgetting. I started to apologize, but... "You know, it's been a busy hour. I got the call about two seconds before I interrupted a killer in the midst of murdering Gladys."

I glanced at Boone apologetically. He softly panted and smiled back at me. Apparently, he was down with me taking credit for his amazing feats of bloodhound awesomeness. "Good boy," I said, and then cranked the air conditioning up a notch. Gladys was still passed out, so she wouldn't mind if it got a little chilly in the car. And Alex could suck it up.

When we arrived at the Society's headquarters, Gladys jerked awake. And just like before, the period of confusion and disorientation that lasted minutes when I woke was but a second for Gladys.

Bright-eyed, she asked, "What did I miss?"

"Not much," I said. "You feeling better?"

"Oh, yes. Just fine. I suppose they'll lock me up while you sort out the details and catch the real killer?"

Her tone was so matter-of-fact that it took me a second to process what she was asking. I stared and tried to think of an answer while Alex went around and opened the door for her.

"They won't lock you up," Alex said, "but you'll need to stay with Anton for a little while to make sure you're safe."

"And that I don't run away." She stepped out of the Jeep, hair in place and sundress unrumpled, looking like there'd been no altercation at all. She hardly appeared the victim of a recent assault.

"That, too," Alex said in an agreeable tone.

I closed my eyes and wondered if vamps ever got headaches, or if I was just imagining the thudding in my brain. I stepped out of the Jeep and hurried to join them. When I caught up, I said, "Everything will be fine. We'll get this sorted out."

"Oh, I know." And Gladys gave me a brilliant smile.

I sighed. She had more faith in me than I had in myself.

❧

CORNELIUS WAS FURIOUS. His eyes went all silver, and I was pretty sure it wasn't a show this time. And he hadn't offered us a seat.

"What were you thinking?" His words were quiet and precise.

"That you'd hang Gladys without blinking, and she didn't do it."

I stared at Cornelius in bewilderment. Had those words just come out of my mouth? Dangit, they had. I shot Alex a nasty look. Where was his shin kicking when it would actually be useful?

At least Gladys wasn't here to see the fallout of my misspoken words. Anton had carted her off once we'd entered the "Employees Only" area, ostensibly for a refreshing drink. Mostly he'd been getting her out of the way so Cornelius could ream us.

Suddenly, I realized what exactly *refreshing* meant. Gladys was off for a quick nip of blood. My stomach roiled.

"Do *not* soil my carpet." Cornelius's icy voice snapped

me out of the death spiral that imagining Gladys drinking nasty, clotted, metallic— I gagged.

Alex kicked me in the shin.

I glared at him then said to Cornelius, "I won't." Between the pain in my shin and the churning of my stomach, my voice came out small and shaky. I barely recognized it as my own.

"Enough—we need to make an attempt to retrieve Becky," Alex said. "You have Gladys in temporary custody, you're aware of Dyson's death and can make the necessary arrangements regarding his position, and I'll ensure the body is delivered as soon as can be arranged so you can examine him yourself."

"Today," Cornelius said. "You will have him delivered today. And I know quite well where the body is located. There is only one place, one person, you'd trust with such a task."

In a tight, steely voice, Alex said, "No harm comes to her. She did nothing wrong."

My stomach and nerves had settled enough for me to catch a hint of lavender in Alex's eyes. He was pissed. Seriously angrily. I took a discreet step to the side, putting a little space between us. If he was going to do some weird wizardy stuff, I didn't want to get caught in the crossfire. Especially since I didn't know exactly what Alex was capable of.

"No harm so long as she delivers the body promptly."

Alex glanced at me, and the glow faded. "We're leaving." Turning to Cornelius, he said, "I'll arrange for Dyson's body to be delivered. No action is to be taken against Gladys until we return. We're going to find Becky."

Cornelius gave Alex a curt nod, and I practically ran through the door.

Alex strode down the hall, and I trotted beside him to

keep up. The guy could cover some ground when he was motivated.

A nasty thought occurred. "What if we can't find Becky?"

"We're screwed." And he picked up his pace even more.

At least we'd stashed Boone in Alex's office before meeting with Cornelius. I did not see a meeting between the hound and his partner's killer going very well. If we did actually find her.

17

LETTERS AND LOCKS

Access to Becky's place was only possible through the main house. So after Alex parked, we hoofed it to the front door. I expected him to pound on it until someone answered. Nope. He rang the doorbell...once.

As I fidgeted and imagined what we'd do if we caught up to the notorious Becky, Alex kept his cool. Typical. I supposed that she would be long gone, but even doing a search of a viable suspect's house seemed pretty exciting to me.

As I bounced on my toes, the door opened. Perfect porcelain skin, gorgeous waves of thick, dark brown hair, and wide hazel eyes—a vision of splendid womanhood opened the front door. Of course. This had to be Rachael.

I stepped to the side so I could get a peek at Alex.

"Rachael."

"Alex."

Rachael smiled at me and said, "You must be Mallory. It's nice to meet you. I'm only sorry it's under such circumstances."

And then I remembered that this woman had no idea

her father was dead. I nodded in reply, uncertain what to say.

"I have news of your father—"

"He's dead. I've known it on some level since he missed his appointment with Cornelius, but I received confirmation shortly before you arrived." Her features softened. "Anton called."

I couldn't believe my eyes. This gorgeous, poised, accomplished woman and *Anton*? I didn't know her, but I was already certain she was too good for the dour grump that I knew.

"Yes." That was all Alex said. He just agreed with her and nothing else.

I stepped closer and nudged him with my elbow.

He frowned at me then said, "I'm sorry for your loss."

Her lips tightened, but that was the only indication she'd heard his expression of condolence. "Mother's out for the day at the spa. She hasn't heard...doesn't know..." Rachael's chin lifted a fraction. "How can I help you?"

These two clearly had weighty history, so I jumped in. "We'd like a chat with Becky. Do you think we could just head on down to the guesthouse?"

But that apparently wasn't a "done" thing, to let one's guests escort themselves, so Rachael took us through the house, down the hill in the backyard to the cottage located in the back.

Where we found the front door ajar.

And me with no Tangwystl. I could smack myself.

A soft whoosh pulled my gaze to Alex and the sword he'd drawn from thin air. I really did need to ask him how he managed to stash that blade.

"Rachael, go back to the house and call emergency

response." Alex stepped in between me and the open door. "Tell them what's happening, and stay in the house."

Once she'd left—which she did without any hesitation —I said, "What am I? Chopped liver?" Because of the two of us, it seemed like Rachael might actually be the harder to kill. Everyone made such a fuss over the hardiness of golems...none of that talk of hardiness extended to vamps.

Without looking at me, Alex stepped into the house. All of his attention was focused ahead. "Not chopped liver; a stubborn nitwit."

I was following him into a dangerous situation, sans magical sword and bubbling over with excitement. He might be right.

It was a small house and didn't take long to clear. The bedroom was the last room we entered, but I knew in the hallway. The smell. Putrid, though it was still fresh with metallic overtones.

En route to the Dyson family home, I'd given some thought to what we would do if we found Becky. What I hadn't considered was finding Becky's dead body.

Her headless, bloody dead body.

Her body lay on the floor near her bed, but her head was several feet away.

With my thumb and forefinger pinching my nose, I said, "I'm surprised there's not more blood." There really wasn't much; just pinching my nose was keeping my stomach happy enough. I was pretty sure the only reason the room stank of the stuff was because it was a relatively small space.

Alex didn't take his eyes from the scene. "Magical sword."

"Why are we sure Rachael didn't do this?"

And then Alex did turn to look at me. "Are we?"

I snorted—which didn't work out so well with my nose

pinched. "*You* are. You seem confident she's actually calling emergency response right now."

Alex turned back to the scene. "Pretty sure she is. I know Rachael pretty well. She didn't do this."

"How can you know her so well and not ever have met her mother?"

"Would you introduce me to your mother?" He started to carefully pick through the contents of the half-packed bag on Becky's bed.

I didn't get where he was coming from. Why would I not introduce him to my mother? "Mom would love you."

"What?" He started to pull clothes out of the bag. "Hey, I think Becky had a tropical destination in mind. Three bikinis, a few sarongs, sundresses, sandals. What about your mom?"

I rolled my eyes. "Nothing. What does Becky's escape destination tell us about her killer?"

"No clue, but it's information. What else do you see?"

I looked around the room. Her bedroom reminded me of mine pre-transformation. Sparse, clean, and nicely decorated. "She's a neat freak?" Then I realized what Alex was saying. "Ah. No struggle. You think she knew her killer?"

"That or it was someone stealthy, and they got the jump on her."

"The only assassins and thieves I know are Anton and Cornelius. Anton is seriously stealthy. And much as I'd like to think Mr. Clean is the baddie here, I'm pretty sure he's not our guy." But then I felt bad. Because if Anton was our killing machine on a spree, that meant he'd be hung.

Okay, I only felt a little bad. He really wasn't nice to me. I unplugged my nose to see if my stomach was up to the task now that my brain had gotten used to the idea of a dead body not far away. The putrid smell filled my nose—nope.

"No. Especially since we just saw him at headquarters."

"Huh?" Preoccupation with settling my stomach had driven our conversation from my brain. Then I remembered: Anton. "Oh, yeah. That would rule him out. Sorry, he's just such an unpleasant guy, my mind had to go there." My hand dropped away from my nose as an inspiring thought occurred, but I plugged it back up only a split second later. "Ophelia. I keep telling you, something is off about that woman. We need to find out if she was actually at that spa. She's a bad apple."

What if I'd been right all along? I had to stop myself from dancing a little jig. That just seemed wrong in the presence of a decapitated body. But the buzz of an answer just around the corner, so, so close, made excitement bubble up inside me. Especially if that answer was the woman I'd been suspicious of from the get-go. It was a little like drinking a few cups of coffee—but more effervescent.

"Mallory."

I looked at Alex, who seemed a little frazzled. Oops. "Yes?"

"Why don't you have a look for another bewitched rope? Or maybe some indication of her travel plans?" Alex crossed his arms. His sword was either sheathed and invisible or returned to whatever place he stashed it. A real mystery, that sword. "Maybe try the kitchen or the study."

"What's got you in a tizzy?"

"I'm not in a tizzy, but you're practically vibrating, and it's distracting. Really annoying, actually." When I hesitated —because dead body and clues really seemed to be in the bedroom—he added, "Besides, that'll get you away from the blood."

"Sold." I made a beeline for the kitchen. The kitchen

was where the action was. People met in the kitchen, chatted in the kitchen, did work at the kitchen table.

Except maybe not in Becky's house. After five minutes, I was pretty sure the kitchen was a bust. Nothing but condiments and take-out leftovers in the fridge; every surface sparkled with cleanliness and lacked any of the clutter that might indicate frequent use. No old mail, no notepad or pen, and no sign that electronics were charged in the area, like a laptop or cell cord left lying around.

Time to scope out the study. After a last peek in Becky's very well-organized but bare cupboards, I headed that way.

"Kitchen's pretty bare," I said to Alex as I walked in the chic but well-used room. Here was the heart of Becky's house.

He was already shuffling through papers on her desk. "Did you do something with the..." What *was* a delicate way to say headless body?

"I've got her wrapped up and ready for emergency response." He frowned then pulled his phone out and dialed. After a second or two, he said, "Where are you?" And then, "Got it." He pocketed his cell phone and said, "They're coming up the drive now."

My curiosity was piqued. I'd only ever met two emergency responders, Alex and Anton. I started to inch toward the door.

"Mallory?"

"Hm?"

I turned to find Alex flipping through paperwork on Becky's desk. "You want to look through this while I try to find her laptop?"

"Right. Of course." I snuck a glance out to the hall then sat down at Becky's desk. Examining the surface, I found it was still tidy but work was in progress. There was a small stack of unopened mail that I flipped through, but nothing stood out. "I suppose we're probably breaking all sort of laws, right?"

"Yeah. Why?" Alex knelt in front of what looked like a small safe.

"Whoa—how did you find that?"

He just looked at me.

"Right. So, since we're doing all this illegal stuff—I mean, you're about to crack her safe, right?" He nodded, and I continued. "So, it's not really that big of a deal that I'm about to break a federal law and open her mail?"

Alex cracked a smile. "I think that's the least of your concerns."

"Right. Just checking." I ripped open the first innocuous envelope, but also kept half an eye on Alex as he did his lock whispering—or was it loosening? Either way, it only took him a flash and the small safe opened.

"That is a really handy skill." I couldn't help but be impressed.

Alex cocked an eyebrow. "For a thief—yes."

He really was a downer today. "How about for an investigator trying to make sure the right person swings for multiple murders?" I didn't say shame on you, but it was implied. He needed to take a little more pride in his work and special talents.

I studied him while his dark head was bent over the safe's contents. He'd been as motivated as me through this whole case. Maybe more. He'd devoted most of his time and energy to finding the guilty party since Dyson's dead body had showed up. He was discontented with the Society's archaic procedures and rules but realistic about the pace of change. He just kept trying to do the right thing.

"You know, Alex, you're a really decent guy."

"What are you talking about?" He looked up at me like I was short a full deck.

True, that had come out of nowhere, but it seemed that he was especially critical of any positive comment I made about him.

"Nothing. What did you find?"

He lifted his hand and I saw that a rope dangled from his fingers.

"Seriously? I thought you said those things were rare?"

"They aren't easy to find, but if you can find a witch who can make them, they typically create them in batches. My guess is that Becky stole part of a batch from headquarters."

"Knowing she couldn't overpower her victims, she snatched them and stashed them for future use." Something was wrong with that equation. "But she didn't use one on Dyson... I'm super confused."

"Yeah. And I thought the other murders were all cover-up murders for the greater crime: Dyson's premeditated murder." Alex set the rope to the side and pulled out a gun, a packet of papers, a necklace, and a small wooden box.

"Hey, boss." A short, broadly muscular man stood in the doorway.

My heart leapt into my throat.

As I tried to catch my breath, Alex stood up and approached the guy in the doorway. As he walked by, he said, "You don't have vamp hearing, either, do you?"

I scowled at his back as he passed, but then my gaze meandered over to the pile of goodies Alex had abandoned. Meet a new enforcer guy or catch a sneak peek of possible evidence? I supposed the evidence could wait an extra minute. I was getting a *little* better at delayed gratification.

"Hi." I waved at the short, stocky guy.

He grinned at me, revealing a charming gap in his front teeth. "Hey, new vamp lady."

There was something genuine and appealing about the man.

"Hey, enforcer guy." I edged closer to the doorway, but I still had to speak around Alex. "I'm Mallory."

"Francis. Good to finally meet you, Mallory. We've all been wondering who's been keeping the boss so busy." He turned back to Alex. "We've got her loaded up, and we're headed back to HQ. Dyson should be on site when we return. Star had to finish up with a client and then was headed to Austin."

"Then get Becky back to HQ and they can double up on autopsies. I assume they're going to have a second look at Dyson."

"Star's the best, but she wasn't working for the Society when she evaluated the corpse—so yes." Francis hesitated, then added, "Lucy's assigned."

"Good grief," Alex said. "She's a child."

"Not anymore, old man; time is sliding past you. But you're right that she isn't as experienced as Star."

"Yeah, we'll see if she can confirm Star's estimated time of death." Alex nodded. "All right. Get out of here. And try not to get a speeding ticket while you're toting around a decapitated corpse."

"I'll do my best, boss." Francis grinned at me again. "Nice to meet you, Mallory."

I gave him a little farewell salute. It seemed appropriate. After he was gone, I asked, "So what is Francis?"

"Always so worried about what enhancements people have."

"Well, until someone lets me know how I can tell us all

apart from each other, then I'm going to keep asking." Just seemed like common sense to me.

"You can't tell from appearance, though there are some general rules of thumb."

"Golems are usually attractive."

Alex nodded. "But otherwise, it's a feel you develop for the magic."

What magic? If this was like the rope thing, then I was screwed. "Oh! Can I open the box?"

Alex bit back a grin. "Sure, you can open the box."

I adored that about the man—he could follow my thoughts down perverse or disjointed paths effortlessly.

As I settled cross-legged on the floor with the box in front of me, I asked, "Is Francis a djinni?"

Alex picked up the packet of papers from the floor, but he didn't join me on the plush rug covering the study floor. "Djinni? Why do you say that?"

"Process of elimination."

"And yet further evidence your precognition skills are nonexistent. Assassin."

I thought back to Francis's gap-toothed grin. "Huh, I wouldn't have guessed such a cheerful soul was an assassin." Then again, Cornelius was the only other one I knew.

"It's almost impossible to tell enhancements from external appearance." He turned back to the stack of handwritten papers and started to read the top one.

Which brought me back to my little box. I picked it up—it didn't weigh much. I was about to flip the lid open when a nasty vision of me and Alex being blown up came to mind. "You're sure this thing isn't booby-trapped?"

"It's fine." Alex was engrossed, his eyes not leaving the page as he spoke to me.

"Hmm. If I get blown up..." I flipped the lid open.

Inside was a lock of hair. A fiery, bright, orangey-red lock of hair. "Ophelia?"

Alex waved the letter he'd been reading. "I'd say yes. This is a letter from Becky to Ophelia. They're all from Becky."

"Why would Becky have letters that she wrote to someone else? Did she never send them?"

"Or got them back somehow." Alex was scanning another of the letters.

"I am so confused."

"Becky and Ophelia were lovers. Does that clear it up?"

"Whaaaaat? Where did that come from?" I looked down at the contents of the box. "Oh. A love token?"

"Maybe. More likely a binding of some kind. Although, if it was a binding, it didn't work." He lifted the paper he'd been reading. "But these are definitely love letters."

"Ah. *That* I didn't expect. And that means that Becky wasn't in love with Dyson."

"Apparently not."

I considered that bit of news. "Okay. Ophelia wants her husband dead for whatever reason, and—"

"Lost social status, for one." Alex shrugged. "It's a thing. He was running the enhanced community in Austin, which also happens to be the hub of enhanced activity in Texas, and then decides to retire...If Rachael wasn't the only one who knew, if Ophelia knew of her husband's pending retirement, then maybe she was pissed about that."

I reached inside the box, but Alex stopped me. "I wouldn't. Could be a token; could be a physical representation of a binding." He reached over and flicked the top of the box. It closed with a decisive click. "You wouldn't want to touch it if it's the second."

When he mentioned binding, I flashed on that moment

when we'd pinky-sworn to keep each other's secrets. Sparks had flown. "A binding, huh? How would that prevent her death?" Death and bindings...bindings and me and Alex... I lowered my voice. "I'm not going to go up in a ball of flames, am I?"

Alex quirked an eyebrow. "Let's not find out."

"Come on. I'm not going to spill your secret. I'm just saying, death wasn't on the table when I pinky-swore with you. I mean, we're talking a pinky swear, like I did when I was a kid. A non-magical, normal kid."

"What we did wouldn't normally create a binding. That's not how it usually works, because intent from both parties is required. Typically. But with you, nothing seems to be typical."

I didn't really get his point, because we were both *intending* to honor a promise. Voila, intent. But then again, there was a lot about this new magical world I didn't quite get. As for not being normal? If I obsessed over everything that wasn't typical in the enhanced community and occurred to or because of me—I'd be bonkers with anxiety.

"Look," Alex said, "all I'm saying is that if I'd entered a magically binding agreement with a co-conspirator, you better believe I'm hedging my bets against assassination." Alex stopped speaking then spun around and drew his sword in one smooth motion. Pretty talented, given the length of the sword, the enclosed space, my proximity, and generally all of the not-very-favorable logistics.

Maybe I *should* do my sword training with Alex.

Then I saw why he'd drawn his sword: Ophelia.

"Poor little lovesick Becky did try to protect herself...but poorly." Ophelia stood in the doorway, casually dressed in skinny jeans and a flowing top, one that allowed great freedom of movement for her sword arm. "Carelessness will happen when one becomes emotionally involved."

She was holding what must be the magical sword that had decapitated Becky. One could only assume poor, lovesick Becky's affections had not been returned. Ophelia seemed the type to use sex to her advantage without becoming emotionally involved. But then again, I'd think anything bad of the woman at this point.

Alex stepped in front of me, which was handy, since I had no weapon. I really needed to improve in that particular area. Walking out the door? Check. Potential danger? Check. Then bring Tangwystl. It wasn't exactly rocket science.

Having Alex's skilled sword arm between me and Ophelia also gave me some time to digest the "co-conspirator" theory. The long and short of it was that Becky might have been the killer and responsible for the deaths of Dyson and Celia, as well as the attempt on Gladys's life, but Ophelia was the brains. And Becky's executioner.

"I knew it," I muttered, and peeked around Alex to get a good look at her. She had evil wench written all over her. And not just now, post-confession. The woman had been flaunting her guilt before. It hadn't been my imagination. I really needed to trust my instincts more. Except my instincts had hardly imagined Becky and Ophelia as co-conspirators.

"I was rather hoping to maintain my alibi at the spa and retrieve those documents—but the timeline was a little too tight. I can't whisper locks like a wizard, and Becky changed the combination." She looked mildly regretful, but otherwise not particularly put out.

I really did not like this woman.

"Please tell me you can kick her ass," I said to Alex. I hadn't forgotten the much-espoused hardiness of golems. "Just have to slice her head off, right?"

I inched further away from Alex when his feet started to move. Being in the crossfire—or within blade range—during a sword fight seemed unwise.

"Oh, Alex can beat me in a fair fight, no problem at all." Ophelia gave Alex a feline smirk. "But I don't fight fair." She reached inside her back pocket and pulled out a small tube. It looked like something from a chem lab.

I had a nasty feeling about that tube. Really nasty. My scalp prickled, and my stomach roiled. *This* was precognition; I was sure of it.

Alex, on the other hand, didn't look very concerned. "You can't poison me."

"Oh? But what about your precious little baby vamp?"

I could feel the tension snap in the air. My vamp radar tingled. That wasn't tension; that was magic. Her threats were a bunch of blah, blah, blah. That tube, on the other hand...

"Alex, I don't think we want to play around with what's inside that thing."

Ophelia uncorked the tube with a flick of her thumb. "Probably not. But you don't have much choice. I have my priorities, and you have yours. Since the cover-up has blown up, I've been working on an escape plan. I need a few days' head start, which will let me disappear." She shrugged. "If you're both alive, then I won't have those few days—will I? But..." She visibly perked up. "Once you're both gone, it will take days for emergency response to piece together the full story. I'll be long gone—along with the remainder of the family estate, naturally."

"You have got to be kidding me," I said, inching to the right. "This was all about the cash?"

"You naïve thing. You are a fluffy little bunny, aren't you?" Ophelia tilted the tube playfully, using it to emphasize her point. "It's always about the cash. Status is of some concern, but more pressing was my dead husband's insistence that he was still capable of running the family's business affairs."

"But Becky was doing that." I thought. That was what Rachael had said.

Alex lunged, his blade moving in for a torso strike.

With a neat bit of footwork, Ophelia blocked the blade, spun, and splashed Alex with the tube's contents. She laughed as she backed away.

Alex advanced, as confident as before—even though my vamp-precog radar was shouting out a warning.

"You should know poisons have practically no effect on me," he said as he made a torso strike.

She parried and nimbly turned. Still she remained on the defensive—waiting.

He struck again, this time forgoing a body shot and scoring a small wound on her upper arm. Blood trickled sluggishly from the cut.

She seemed not to notice it. "Practically? But no matter, since that was no poison." She parried another advance from Alex, looking much too confident for someone who should be outclassed. "A basic brew, one every little witchling can make." She parried again. "An inebriation potion. Simple, harmless, popular at high school parties. And such an innocuous concoction that it won't trigger your natural and mystical protections, wizard." She snapped out the last word like an epithet.

The tip of Alex's blade dropped and he backed away, yanking his shirt over his head. He flung it into a corner, his eyes never leaving Ophelia. "How?" A note of panic rang in his voice. "How did you know?"

I was far enough to his right that I could see the glinting

lavender of his eyes. Uh, out-of-control, glowing eyes were kinda my thing. I'd known that tube was bad news—but this...this was unexpected.

I could feel my chest tightening.

I'd never seen Alex's eyes turn full-on, glowing lavender. Never heard him panicked, either. And he wasn't trying to hide his tatts. Since I was pretty sure they were a secret, or shameful in some way... Yeah, this was super bad.

Ophelia smiled again. "Your secrets aren't as secret as you might wish, wizard."

Alex lunged again. He seemed as graceful, as coordinated, as proficient as before. I wasn't sure why he'd sounded so frightened.

Ophelia met his attack and backed away. "Your little vamp pet doesn't know, does she?" She didn't attack. At a guess, I'd say she was stalling.

As I watched, a tattoo that ran parallel to Alex's spine glimmered. "Alex, your tattoo—"

"I know." His voice sounded strained as he made yet another attack. But Ophelia wasn't engaging. She was handy with her sword, strong, probably quite proficient. At least from what little knowledge I'd gained in my lessons, it appeared that way. And she was definitely stalling.

His voice edgy, Alex said, "Mallory, if I try to hurt anyone but Ophelia..."

"Losing control already? You poor man. You should have been more careful as a boy. Those who play with demons will be possessed, won't they?"

Oh, no. Now I got it. Alex didn't drink, didn't go without sleep, exercised, ate well—and not because he couldn't tolerate a little nasty whispering in his ear on a bad day.

"Alex?" And now I sounded like the panicked rabbit

Ophelia had named me earlier. I squared my shoulders and in a firmer voice said, "Alex, what do I do?"

"If I'm possessed?" He shot me a quick glance, and his eyes blazed purple. "If I try to hurt anyone but this murderous bitch, kill me."

And I wanted to cry, because he meant it. And then I didn't want to cry, because even if I could hurt him, I didn't have my dang magical sword. Not to defend myself. Not to defend him.

I was an idiot.

A nasty crawling sensation creeped along my skin. Something was here. Something vile.

And I didn't even have my sword.

"Tangwystl!" The scream was torn from my throat.

18

POSSESSED

That familiar, paradoxical feeling of lightness and heft filled my hand: Tangwystl. I wrapped my fingers around her hilt.

I didn't think how, I just turned instinctively to the threat...only I turned to Alex, not Ophelia. His eyes blazed purple, and the tattoo on his back shone so brightly that I could see the shimmer when facing him head on.

Bad. Very bad.

I was trapped in the corner with not even a window exit. Ophelia had retreated to the hallway, but she hadn't left. She watched, waiting for...what, exactly?

Alex's features hardened, his lip lifted, and he groaned. It wasn't even Alex's voice, but a disgusting, perversion of the deep, sometimes gruff voice I knew.

"Alex?"

"It can't speak. It feels. Hungers, lusts, hates. But the thing inside him can't speak." Ophelia didn't look quite so self-satisfied as she had earlier.

"What did you do to him?" But I didn't need her to answer. I knew what she'd done. She'd made him weak. So weak that some nasty creature had taken up residence inside his body. Looking for any sign of the man I knew, I said, "Alex, I know you're there somewhere."

I knew that Alex could communicate with the spirits he encountered, so why couldn't the thing inside him talk? Even if Alex couldn't reach through whatever control the creature had on him, why didn't it speak?

Ophelia started to slip away. I wasn't sure what she expected: that we'd kill each other? Or had she simply not expected Alex to function with that thing inside him?

"Look." I pointed at Ophelia with the tip of my sword.

Alex turned.

And that was when I noticed his sword. It was gone. Vanished. If he'd dropped it, it would be at his feet, but it was nowhere to be seen.

I just sicced a weaponless, possessed Alex on Ophelia. I was incredibly bad at this. I really needed an instruction manual for how to be a better ninja-sleuth-vamp.

What could I do? Distract. Evade. Get that thing out of him. Ophelia was a secondary problem at this point.

I smacked Alex on the rear with the flat on my sword. Not something I'd actually ever practiced, but I figured it would get his attention.

And it did. He turned to me with an unfamiliar look of intent interest on his face. Not good. Very not good.

"Tangwystl, I really need you to play replica sword right now. Like in training, no sharp parts."

Tangwystl blew a raspberry.

"Right now; I'm serious," I whispered in a strained voice. Ophelia had been slowly inching away, but when Alex turned his attention to me, she'd darted out of sight. "Now."

She sighed, made a spitting noise, but finally agreed. *No slicing.*

"You lovely little girl." And then I beat the leering Alex-but-not-Alex with my now relatively safe sword.

I got his forearms, shoulder, missed a kick to the junk, and finally managed a blow to the head—"I'm so sorry, Alex"—and that made him groan, duck, and bend enough that I could run past him.

And I ran. Like a crazed vamp out for revenge. Which I was. This lady had messed with my client, gotten Alex possessed, and masterminded the death of two people. Bad golem lady, bad.

Looked like I had some decent vamp speed when my stress levels were through the roof. Party for me...or not.

"Give me an edge, Tangwystl."

Weeeeeeee

I took that as a yes, and attacked.

Turned out weaponry mattered. More than skill, in this instance. And my magical living sword was better than her magical not-living sword. Three blows and I shattered the lesser blade. Good thing, too, because I wasn't sure I could last much more than that with my less-than-perfected sword skills.

I practically wept in relief when her blade failed.

Then I took her head.

It was over so fast, I didn't know what to think. The fiery red strands of her long hair wrapped around the unevenly rolling ball her head had become, and I watched it wobble its way several feet down the drive before it stopped.

Then the smell of blood hit me.

My nose filled with the putrid stench, and I threw up. I tried really hard to miss her decapitated body. Really I did.

But I couldn't linger over the mess or feel terribly sorry about not quite missing her entirely—because I had a possessed partner to save. I felt a little guilty that Rachael might find her mother's body in that particularly undignified position—but the woman was a crazy killer lady. Nothing much less dignified than that, and Rachael seemed a practical sort of kid. I hoped.

When I hoofed it back to the cottage, I retraced my steps around the side of the house. And much as I tried to will myself to vamp up the speed, I was pretty certain I only managed a slow to middling human jog. Not drinking blood had major disadvantages, and my inability to turn on the vamp speed ninety-nine percent of the time seemed to be one of them.

"Tangwystl? Pretty please, take away the edge. If you're quick and don't argue, I promise to start training with Wembley and Alex." If Alex survived.

Wahoo! Einarr slices dices most best. Best ever. Superhero strong.

And then she sighed a gusty girl-crush sigh.

My sword crushing over Einarr, a.k.a. Wembley, was too much for me to digest at the moment. But I would be revisiting that disturbing thought. One thing was sure: she had no idea how little her buddy "Einarr" had been training the last century or so. I didn't have the heart to tell her that he was actually pretty terrible these days. She'd find out soon enough. Assuming the demon—or Alex possessed by the demon—didn't put a permanent end to my newly acquired vamp existence.

I opened the front door and made a cautious entry.

I lifted my once again dull sword and whispered, "Thanks, pretty girl."

She made a smooching noise at me.

I really didn't get Alex's issue with living swords. I adored Tangwystl. Who wanted a boring old sword with no personality? And apparently living metal rocked it against the regular magical stuff.

"Alex?" I called out. Because that was a good idea with a possessed guy around the corner.

I lifted my sword and barely refrained from beating myself over the head with it for my stupidity.

When I didn't find him in the living room, I headed back to the study. I really didn't want to get trapped back there with him in his current state, but I also couldn't leave him unchecked to ramble through the neighborhood, doing who knew what.

What *exactly* would he do?

I sped up.

At least he wasn't armed. I almost tripped over my own feet, because of course he was armed. The gun in the safe. How could I have forgotten the gun?

And then I ran toward the study. Everything in me said *hurry*. Nothing said wait, be cautious, you might be shot. Precognition; I'd stake my life on it.

As I ran straight into the study, I realized—belatedly—that I was.

19

GREEN GANGSTER GHOULY

Alex held the gun to his head.

His eyes blazed purple, but they were his eyes...mostly.

"It's still here." He was huddled in a corner of the room on the floor, knees drawn up to his chest, the tattoo on his back flush against the wall.

I let Tangwystl's tip rest against the floor.

"It may still be here, but you're here, too. That's a pretty big improvement over just a few minutes ago."

A tortured look crossed his face. "What did I do?"

"You didn't do anything. Whatever it is inside of you, it didn't get a chance to hurt a fly." I left out the part about me beating him about the head and shoulders. He could blame me for any head trauma after we got that nasty thing out of him. "Any recs on getting rid of your visitor?"

Alex pushed the barrel of the gun against his head.

"No." I tried not to hyperventilate and kept my face and voice as calm as I could. "No, that's a bad idea, Alex. I don't think a wizard could survive that."

He let his head fall back against the wall, but the gun stayed pressed against his temple. "That's the idea, Mallory." He looked exhausted. Bone-deep, can't-stand-another-moment tired.

My eyes started to burn.

And Alex cracked a smile. "Only you would cry at a time like this." As he spoke, the glow in his eyes died.

I was pretty sure that wasn't true *at all*, but I let it slide. I dabbed at my eyes on my T-shirt, and when I looked at Alex again I could see it.

A greenish wisp in and around his body. The image of the creature was superimposed over Alex—but it was also as if Alex had absorbed some of that mist.

"I can see it." I said it quietly, as if the admission would startle the creature into action.

With his head still resting against the wall and the barrel against his temple, he shook his head slowly. "You can never let anyone know about that."

"You've got to be kidding me. We have way bigger issues right now." I laid Tangwystl on the floor, well away from Alex. Suicide by sword seemed awkward and unwieldy, but Alex was acting pretty motivated right now. If I did manage to get that gun away from him, it'd be just my luck he'd grab Tangwystl. I nudged her further away with my toe.

As I walked closer to Alex, his eyes darted away. He couldn't hold my gaze.

"Does all the sex have something to do with keeping these things away?" I asked him as I inched closer.

"Seriously?" He gave me an incredulous look, and the barrel angled away slightly. "You're asking me that now?"

I'd always wondered, but mostly I was asking to distract him. I really wanted the answer to an entirely different question. "Why not? You have a gun to your head. I may not ever find out if I don't ask now."

He made an exasperated sound. "I don't go hungry, I stay in decent shape, and I have sex often enough that I don't feel like I'm abstaining. It's just about keeping a healthy balance for all appetites. Don't glut and don't abstain."

"Really? You seem to get around a lot."

I kept my eye on the wispy green edges. What I really wanted to know—more than the details of Alex's full or balanced or whatever sex life—was whether I could touch that misty green vapor.

Alex turned his head away from me, the barrel of the gun pointed to the ground, and I grabbed that nasty piece-of-garbage demon and yanked as hard as I could.

And fell back on the floor—with the misty, horny beast on top of me.

"Ack! Get off me, you sick puppy."

I scrambled backward on hands and elbows and butt and smacked my head hard against the wall. "Owww!"

By the time I'd stopped rubbing the sting from my scalp, the thing had gone. Faded from my sight, at least. I looked around the room and couldn't find a trace of it.

Alex still looked exhausted and still sat propped against the wall in the corner a few feet away, but he'd set the gun aside. "How in the world did you know to do that? That you even *could* do that?"

"Not a flipping clue." I stood up, grinning broadly. "Precognition?" I said it mostly to annoy him, and offered him a hand up.

Alex snorted and took my hand.

I hauled him to his feet, and he wobbled for a second. When he was steady, I let go of his hand.

"Maybe the question of precog enhancements requires a little more study." He rubbed the side of his head. "Do you know what happened to me? I feel like I've been hit by a car."

"Yeah, about that..."

20

AND THAT'S HOW IT WAS DONE

For once, I drove. Alex was hardly in a state to walk a straight line, let alone drive. Although he'd had the presence of mind to grab the necklace and letters from the safe as we'd been leaving, as well as the bewitched rope. The box he'd left conspicuously behind, but he had returned it to the safe.

I texted emergency response with the cleanup request and 9-1-1 while Alex climbed into the car. Shirtless. That's how exhausted he was. His tattoos were there for all the world to see, and he didn't seem to care.

I started the Jeep. The faster we were both home, the better.

"I should feel a little bad about leaving a decapitated body in the driveway."

Alex leaned his head back against the headrest and closed his eyes. "But you don't."

"Nah. The property is private enough that no one should see it unless the neighbors come calling. And emergency response should be here in fifteen minutes or so. Rachael, though—"

"There's no love lost between mother and daughter."

"Well, there you go." I gave Ophelia's headless body a jaunty wave on the way out. If anyone ever deserved to have her head lopped off, Ophelia did. "Poor Becky."

Alex huffed in surprise. "You're kidding. She killed two people and was trying to kill a third when you interrupted her."

"But she did it for love, right? A messed up, twisted, not-reciprocated love—sure. But Ophelia pulled all the strings, which in my mind makes her the real murderer, and she did it for the cash. I mean, really, yuck."

"Your moral compass might be a little askew." Alex didn't elaborate as to why, but he didn't need to.

I sighed. He was right. Murder was bad—the worst of the worst—and Becky had murdered not just Dyson, but also Alex's friend. I just couldn't get past Ophelia as the true criminal of the whole thing. I glanced at Alex, and found that he was looking a little better. He'd opened his eyes, anyway, and some of the grayish tinge to his skin was gone. I kept my eyes firmly at neck level and above. He would not appreciate me examining the symbols all over his chest.

My phone rang but I just ignored it. I was driving...and I didn't want to talk to Cornelius or any of the emergency response guys.

"You have the letters. Read them and see if there's any clue as to why Becky fell for that nasty piece of work. She had to know what Ophelia was like, having worked for the woman's husband for donkey's years. Heck, she lived on their property for who knew how long." Although probably not that long, since enhanced humans had that tricky little non-aging thing to deal with.

Alex scooped up the pile of letters from the floor, and

the necklace. The letters he left in his lap, but the necklace he examined. "Well, who would have thought..."

His phone rang, but he declined the call. When I looked to see what he was doing, I found him holding the chain of the necklace and watching the pendant. It swayed gently back and forth with the motion of the car.

He caught my glance and nodded at the pendant. "I think this is our succubus."

"A necklace?"

"Yeah. The Society will have to get Star or one of the other more qualified witches to verify, but I'd wager this little trinket holds what's missing of Dyson's energy. The stone pendant is wicked powerful—full of some kind of magical energy. I didn't notice before, because I only handled the chain."

"Um, kind of a morbid thought." I wrinkled up my nose. "But any chance they can reanimate him with that?"

"Oh, no, I don't think so. I think that would be a little like trying to give a corpse a blood transfusion."

Ick. Icky. Ick. I shook my head, trying to clear the image away.

Once I had a handle on the nauseating roll of my stomach, I said, "So Becky dolls herself up as Gladys and slaps on an illusion to make up the difference—not that hard, because Dyson doesn't actually know the real Gladys. Then she puts this necklace on, and they—what? Do some ritual to draw out his spirit? Because Dyson's not participating in something that's killing him. Not willingly."

Alex laughed, but the sound came out hoarse. "I'd wager this thing requires skin contact. And if so, what better way to get the man in contact with the necklace than a little affair with a gorgeous red-head? Which is how Gladys ended up as their patsy; she was Dyson's type."

I was trying not to get too distracted by the story, because if I didn't pay attention while I was driving, I'd probably give Alex a heart attack...but this was juicy stuff. After a few minutes, I asked what had to be the most obvious question. "Why not chop off his head?"

"Because Ophelia would have been the first suspect. Again, I don't think Dyson died when he was supposed to. I bet Becky and Ophelia thought they had more time to firmly establish the affair."

"I don't know. If there wasn't solid proof of Ophelia's guilt, she wouldn't be executed, right? She's not Gladys; she has standing in the community. I really don't see the point—Whoa, Rachael."

"Yeah. Convince Rachael her dad died in the arms of another woman, and Ophelia is off the hook. Rachael would have been the impetus behind a head-lopping investigation." Alex scratched his jaw. "But how do they make the energy suck look like natural causes? I'm not sure on that part."

"Do they have to? Consider that Dyson dies while having sex with Gladys. Either the cause is unknown, or Gladys killed him. That's the implication, right? So, sure, the crazy killer ladies may have had a way to make the death look natural if their timeline hadn't been sped up, but even if they didn't—I think they get away with it."

"Except they didn't." He dropped the necklace back on the floor, in between his feet.

"Nope. They didn't. A few stray details gone awry—and our timely interference—and voila, mystery solved."

Alex's phone rang again and he silenced it. "Except we were a little late."

"Yeah, I'm really sorry about Celia. Oh, poor Boone. He's been hanging out in your office for an hour or more now.

Can you text Wembley and see if he'll pick him up? I really don't want to see Cornelius right now. I need a little me time before that happens. At the least, a shower."

I'd been trying not to think about it, but a few drops of golem blood had made their way onto my clothes. And the faint odor had amplified inside the closed car. I cracked a window, but I couldn't leave it down, since we were on the freeway.

"I'll just read these, and you focus on not puking."

By the time we arrived back at the house, between the two of us, we'd declined seven calls from Cornelius. But Alex had managed to at least scan most of the letters.

He bundled up the letters in a neat pile. "It looks like Becky was actually in love with Ophelia. So it wasn't a light affair, not on her part, at least. Why is there a cop car in front of your house?"

I was too tired for another police interview, dishy detective or not. "Could they have worse timing? I wish we could just tell them that Mrs. A's killer was long gone." I kept driving past the house. "We need to touch base with Cornelius before I go through another interview with Detective Ruiz. I mean, can't the guy make an appointment?"

I pulled to the curb and dithered for a second over texting or calling. I felt like sending Cornelius a Tangwystl-style raspberry via text. I was pretty sure I could record it and send the sound clip, but Alex put the kibosh on that idea. Not that I would have truly done it. I was mostly sure I wouldn't—but I was a little punchy and overtired.

A phone call was in order, and I knew it. The alternative was Alex calling, and he was in worse shape than me. I scrunched up my face in distaste, then dialed.

Five minutes later, I hung up. That hadn't been so bad. I did tell the Society's CSO and acting CEO to release Gladys immediately or he wasn't ever getting the details about Becky and Ophelia's plot for world domination. I really was tired if I could talk to Cornelius like that.

And while Cornelius was not amused, he said he was immediately releasing Gladys.

As soon as I hung up, I got a text from Gladys: *Thank you! Alex and you are wonderful! I knew you could do it!*

Right. Glad someone had confidence in me. This sleuthing stuff was seriously taxing and not nearly as easy as it looked on TV.

I flashed the screen at Alex, and he grinned when he read it. "At least someone will sleep well tonight."

"All right, time to head home. I need a shake, and you need a shirt. Maybe the cops will let us clean up a little before they grill us over Mrs. A's demise."

THE END

Book 3 in the Vegan vamp series, *The Elvis Enigma*, is releasing December 1, 2016.

BONUS CONTENT

Interested in bonus content for the Vegan Vamp series? Subscribe to my newsletter to receive a bonus chapter for *Adventures of a Vegan Vamp* as well as release announcements and other goodies! Sign up at http://eepurl.com/b6pNQP.

ABOUT THE AUTHOR

Cate Lawley is the pen name for Kate Baray's sweet romances and cozy mysteries, including The Goode Witch Matchmaker and Vegan Vamp series. When she's not tapping away at her keyboard or in deep contemplation of her next fanciful writing project, she's sweeping up hairy dust bunnies and watching British mysteries with her pointers and hounds.

Cate also writes urban and paranormal fantasy as Kate Baray and thrillers as K.D. Baray.

For more information:
www.catelawley.com
www.facebook.com/katebaray
www.twitter.com/katebarayauthor